C000185394

THE INTIMATE MEMOIRS OF
AN EDWARDIAN DANDY
Volume II

The Intimate Memoirs of an Edwardian Dandy

Volume II
An Oxford Scholar

Rupert Mountjoy

Edited and Introduced by
KEVIN PLYMOUTH

WARNER BOOKS

A *Warner* Book

First published in Great Britain in 1992
by Warner Books

Copyright © 1992 by Potiphar Productions

The moral right of the author has been asserted.

*All characters in this publication are fictitious
and any resemblance to real persons, living or dead,
is purely coincidental.*

A CIP catalogue record for this book
is available from the British Library

ISBN 0 7515 0007 0

Photoset in North Wales by
Derek Doyle & Associates, Mold, Clwyd.
Printed in England by Clays Ltd, St Ives plc

Warner Books
A Division of
Little, Brown and Company (UK) Limited
165 Great Dover Street
London SE1 4YA

THE INTIMATE MEMOIRS OF
AN EDWARDIAN DANDY
Volume II

Introduction

FROM THE MIDDLE OF THE NINETEENTH century to approximately one hundred years later sexuality was a taboo subject in Britain.

Whilst the upper classes paid only lip service to the strict and often unpleasantly hypocritical morality urged upon the populace by the then powerful Church and all other organs of the Established order, the world of our great grandparents was one in which an astonishingly high number of people lived in ignorance, their natural feelings numbed and inhibited as Society successfully established stringent control over this area of their lives.

Working class adolescents learned what little they knew from their peers at school or at work, though as Dr Steve Humphries commented pithily in his fascinating book *A Secret World Of Sex: The British Experience 1900-1950*: 'Young people, from whatever background, generally taught each other about the facts of life – though there were strenuous efforts by adults to control their knowledge and keep them in ignorance ... moral reformers constantly complained that poor children knew too much for their own good.

Better-off parents usually exerted greater control over their children's sexual knowledge and development. If a boy or – even more worrying – a girl from a well-to-do background indulged in this kind of sexual experimentation, the parents would usually intervene very rapidly to put an end to it.'

However, in wealthy houses, boys were often not actively discouraged from enjoying their first sexual lessons from female servants, though of course any untoward consequences usually resulted in the girl being thrown out of the door to fend for herself. Often their own families were no less harsh, rejecting their 'wicked' daughters who ended up in either the local workhouse or one of the bleak, spartan homes run by such organisations as the Salvation Army. No doubt, several girls preferred to swell the throngs of 'unfortunates' who crowded the streets of London and other major cities.

Yet is has always been the self-imposed duty of the upper and middle classes to protect the lower orders from their own base instincts. But human nature cannot be denied and recent republication of late Victorian underground erotic novellas such as *The Intimate Memoir of Dame Jenny Everleigh* show that under the all-enveloping public respectability of the age, there was another world peopled by high-spirited consenting adults who revelled in sexual enjoyments.

By the turn of the century, basic adult literacy had almost been fully achieved and amongst the most popular entertainments for young Edwardian men was the 'horn' book, of which

Rupert Mountjoy's salacious autobiography is a typical example. Not only did such books provide sexual stimulation, but they preached a gospel that sexual activity was to be enjoyed, and in addition they provided valuable instruction in sexual techniques and thus offered a platform of resistance to the suffocating guilt-ridden climate in which they originally appeared.

Professor Warwick Jackson gives a thumbnail sketch of Rupert Mountjoy's interesting life in his introduction to the first book of these memoirs: *An Edwardian Dandy 1: Youthful Scandals*, which was published earlier this year. Suffice it to say here that our author enjoyed a typically sybaritic lifestyle of a wealthy young gentleman around the turn of the century, and his many tales of intimate intrigue, clandestine affairs and all the many thrills of lust were further enhanced for himself and his contemporary readers by the spice of prohibition.

These diaries were first published (illicitly, of course, as the explicit, uncensored writing is bawdy even by modern liberal standards) just before the outbreak of World War One, in 1913. Rupert certainly took part in a wide variety of sexual adventures about which he writes with a liveliness which distinguishes his work from certain pale imitators and shows how much he enjoyed his many erotic escapades as he and his friends, male and female, discarded the constraining yoke of the manners and mores of the Edwardian Establishment.

As Rupert Mountjoy himself wrote in 1909 to Heather O'Fluffert, one of the trio of writers who composed the multi-volume *The Intimate Memoir Of Dame Jenny Everleigh* (now also available in a series of paperbacks from Warner Books): 'All animals copulate but only man is capable of extending a physical need into an act of love. This ability sets mankind apart from the lower species, although it is surely a most unfortunate fact that far too few of us recognise and develop this unique talent with which we have all been blessed.

'So many people are being hindered by the lack of open exploration of sexual matters and are cursed by the innate, often hypocritical, prudery in Society that the merest discussion of a morality based upon more reasonable precepts is forbidden. At least there are some of us who strive to formulate a set of ethical principles for the twentieth century that will be based upon a saner understanding of our own natural desires.'

Happily, the original manuscript of Rupert Mountjoy's memoirs was recently discovered and this has afforded us the opportunity to relive his amorous adventures that show to the modern reader a very different side to the starched picture of life in Great Britain some one hundred years ago.

Kevin Plymouth
Ipswich
August,1992

4

Green grow the rushes O,
Green grow the rushes O;
The sweetest hours that e'er I spent,
Were spent among the lasses O!

ROBERT BURNS
(1759-1796)

CHAPTER ONE

A Freshman's Tale

'HERE'S A LITTLE TRICK WHICH WILL amuse the ladies at your party tonight,' said Barry Jacobs, a fellow undergraduate I met during my second week of the Varsity when we were both chosen to play football for the college team on the strength that we had both captained our school elevens at soccer. He was a clever chap and though our life paths took very different directions after leaving Oxford, Barry and I have remained close personal chums. 'Do you have a pencil and paper to hand?

'Listen carefully now, Rupert – take your age and double it; then add five. Right? Now, think of any number between one and ninety-nine; and now take away the number of days in a year. Finally, add one hundred and fifteen and divide by one hundred. Now see where the decimal point comes. Your age will be to the left of it and the number between one and ninety-nine that you chose will be to the right of it! Isn't that amazing?'*

*Alas, this party trick does not seem to work! – Editor.

But dear readers, I feel that I am in too much haste in beginning these recollections of my splendid years spent 'twixt the dreaming spires of the internationally famous University of Oxford, in the heart of England's green and pleasant land. For those of you who have yet to read of my early exploits in the grand *l'arte de faire l'amour* I had best swiftly sketch the bare details of my life so far. [*Rupert Mountjoy's first amorous adventures were republished for the first time in uncensored, explicit form in* An Edwardian Dandy 1: Youthful Scandals – *Editor*].

Although my family seat is in Yorkshire, I attended boarding school down in Sussex at St Lionel's Academy For the Sons Of Gentlefolk. I was initiated into the joys of sensuality, however, by Diana Wigmore, the beautiful daughter of a neighbour and my friend Frank Folkestone (who also crossed the Rubicon during that never-to-be-forgotten summer holiday) and I enjoyed further liaisons at school with Prince Salman of Lockshenstan. Salman, the son of a fabulously wealthy maharajah, liked nothing better than to fuck himself into a stupor at any and every opportunity and the girls of the nearby village queued up to receive his spunky libations and twenty pound notes which he generously distributed to his female companions.

Nevertheless, all play and no work is a recipe for disaster as Dr Keeleigh, our dear old headmaster used to say, and Salman took his wise words to heart. My Indian pal was a diligent scholar and I was sorry that he did not accept the place offered him at University College, Oxford

8

but preferred to continue his scientific studies at Trinity College, Cambridge. However, we did keep in touch from time to time as will be recorded in this narrative.

My other inseparable schoolfellow was Frank Folkestone and to our mutual delight we were both accepted by Balliol College to study law. Our rooms were on the same landing in college which pleased us both and, as will be noted, this arrangement proved to be extremely convenient for, how shall I best put it, our often joint extra mural activities.

Hopefully this will set the scene for you, dear reader. Let us now return to a pleasant day in early October, 1899. I was walking down St Cross Road with Barry Jacobs after we had taken part in an hour's training for the football match against Brasenose College to be played on the following Saturday. It had been a dry, warm summer and the weather had yet to turn cold and walking slowly away from the playing fields I felt at peace with the world. In the quiet lane I thought I could hear some conkers falling and I noticed that the ash-keys were turning gold along with a few adjacent leaves – but all other leaves on the ash-tree boughs were still green. Barry had also been affected by the beauty of our surroundings and he exclaimed: 'We're really lucky chaps to be at Oxford, aren't we Rupert? How did the poet put it:

Towery city and branchy between towers;
Cuckoo-echoing, bell swarmed, lark-charmed, rook-
racked, river rounded;
The dapple-eared lily below thee; . . .'

'Very well said – especially coming from a mathematics scholar!' I joked, 'but frankly I'm thinking of a more down-to-earth matter. I've been invited to a reception this evening given by Doctor Nicholas Blayers at Jesus College. He's a cousin of the headmaster at my old school and probably the most radically minded senior tutor in the entire University. He believes in mixed colleges with boys and girls studying together. Now you know how resistant most Oxonians were to the idea of women being admitted at all and how today their colleges are strictly out of bounds to us.

'Well, because he believes (and quite rightly in my opinion) that undergraduates of both sexes should mix freely without undue hindrance, at his own expense Doctor Blayers is throwing a party for a group of first year female students from Somerville College and a similar number of male freshmen. Now I happen to know that several of these girls have come to Oxford from Trippett's Academy For The Daughters Of Gentlefolk down in the West Country. This is a school run by Dame Agatha Humphrey, the famous champion of higher education for women and frankly, I'm more than a little apprehensive about meeting sophisticated young ladies from there. You attended a day school in London and I doubt whether you can appreciate what a sheltered life one has to live even at a progressive English boarding school like St Lionel's.'

Barry looked at me in some astonishment. 'What on earth have you to be scared about? What a marvellous chance you have to meet some girls – gosh, Rupert, I wish I had been given an invitation to such a spiffing party. I just can't imagine any problem or are you just very shy?'

'Yes, I suppose I am,' I admitted, for with the exception of my initiation into the joys of fucking by Diana and her friend Cecily, along with some uninhibited horseplay with some housemaids at St Lionel's with Frank and Salman, I had little to no experience of social intercourse with the female sex. 'I'm worried that I will find myself quite tongue-tied. How do I continue a conversation with a girl after enquiring about the state of the weather? To be honest, I'm uncertain about what to say next!'

'Now this can often be a thorny problem for boys,' admitted Barry as we trudged along. 'It has to be said that girls are not usually interested in current affairs (except those of an intimate nature!), sport or other masculine pursuits, and we are hardly enraptured by feminine chit-chat. Also, they have been told by their mamas that they must not be too forward in the initiation of conversation with young men and should only speak when spoken to – so this makes the situation even more difficult.

'My solution is to try your luck with subjects such as the weather, gardening, food, the latest plays or the current exhibition at the Royal Academy. This usually works although, of course, I cannot give you a cast-iron guarantee of success. However, just before I came up to Oxford my uncle, Sir Lewis Osborne, invited me to a splendid dinner-party to celebrate the eighteenth birthday of my cousin Philippa. I was sitting next to an extremely attractive girl named Adrienne and I tried my best to impress her with some smart, sophisticated conversation. In vain I went through all the subjects I have just mentioned but I couldn't raise the slightest glimmer of interest. I even tried talking about the magnificent dishes being served which were all strictly kosher [*prepared to Jewish dietary laws – Editor*] but she barely concealed her boredom and was even beginning to yawn.

'At this stage I was frankly ready to throw in the towel but just then a footman approached and handed me a note on a silver salver. "A message from your cousin Philippa, sir," he whispered into my ear. I opened it surreptitiously under the tablecloth and with difficulty deciphered Philippa's scrawl. She had written: *Try Votes For Women*, so I pocketed the scrap of paper and tackled Adrienne again. "What do you think of Mrs Pankhurst and the suffragettes?" I asked and *voila!* instantly into her lovely brown eyes leapt a bright gleam of genuine interest.

'Philippa had noticed how I was struggling and her kind message certainly did the trick for me. Adrienne was an ardent supporter of the emancipation of women and as I have never understood why women should be treated as second class citizens I could honestly put my hand on my heart and tell her that I agreed with every word she said. I told her of my father's letter on the subject which had been published a few weeks back in *The Daily Chronicle*. He had argued that women's suffrage would come once the present social, educational and economic changes now taking place had worked themselves through the system. The choice is not between going on and standing still, it is between advancing and retreating, he had written in his forceful conclusion.

' "Oh, so it was your Papa who wrote that letter," said Adrienne, now flashing a luscious smile at me. "How silly of me not to have realised that Leonard Jacobs was your Papa. I know of his reputation as a generous philanthropist and I am glad to hear that he holds progressive social views."

' "Like his son," I added with a twinkle in my eye and she squeezed my hand as she said: "I'm very glad to hear it." Well, from an unpromising start the evening could hardly have gone better. After dinner we sat and chatted and she even accepted a lift home in my hansom, sending her parents' carriage back, telling the coachman that she had made other arrangements. I escorted her to her front door and she invited me in for a night-cap.'

He paused and I said: 'Well go on, old boy, don't stop there. This sounds like a story with a jolly interesting ending!'

Barry laughed and said: 'Well, it does get a little spicy, Rupert, and I wouldn't want to offend your aesthetic sensibilities. Are you sure you want me to continue?'

'You'd better watch out for your own aesthetic sensibilities if you don't carry on!' I retorted, and so with a grin he continued the tale.

'Well, it was well past midnight when we arrived at her parents' house in Allendale Avenue. Everyone had retired and she told the footman who had waited up for her that he too could now

13

go to bed. She poured out large cognacs which we sipped as we sat together on the sofa. "You know, Barry, it's funny that I did not realise that Leonard Jacobs was your father," she said thoughtfully, "but then we don't always know everything about our parents, do we? Why, only last week I discovered that my own Papa has a collection of sketches by poor Aubrey Beardsley. He has kept them under lock and key in the library but by chance I picked them up the other day. Would you like to see them?" *[Aubrey Beardsley (1872-1898) was a brilliant young illustrator best known for his distinctively stylised work and also for his explicitly rude drawings which scandalised London Society one hundred years ago — Editor].*

' "I certainly would, Adrienne," I said, and she brought over a folder from a bureau in the corner of the room. I opened it and the first picture was of two plump nuns lying naked on a bed working dildoes into their open cunnies. They were being watched by two monks peeping round the door who had thrown up their cassocks and pulled out their pricks, each tossing off the other as they looked upon the lascivious women playing with themselves. The next drawing really made my cock swell up. It showed a beautiful dark-haired girl seated on the lap of her lover. Both were nude and between her thighs you could see that her pussey was engorged with his swollen cockshaft. She had one hand round his neck and in the other she was cupping his hairy ballsack.

'It became quite obvious that Adrienne's blood had also been fired by sight of these erotic drawings. She pressed her thighs together and made no objection when my arm stole round her shoulders and she cuddled into my body as we looked at another illustration of this same couple, only this time the girl was kneeling between his legs, her bottom well stuck out and the furrow in between shown in loving detail. She was shown opening her lips in order to take the shiny knob of the young fellow's stiff lovestick inside her mouth. The next sketch showed her flat on her back with her legs wide open. Her handsome lover was balancing on his forearms above her and this time her cunney was engorged with the thick prick of her lover who had inserted his staff in to the very roots of his pubic hair.

'I could no longer contain my feelings and I burst out: "My God! Wouldn't I give anything to be in his place." I bit my lip as soon as I had uttered this heartfelt but uncouth plea. Surely she would recoil away in disgust! But to my surprise and absolute joy, Adrienne placed her hand directly on my straining cock. She unbuttoned my trousers and brought out my throbbing tool which she stroked gently with her hand, saying with a mischievous chuckle: "Yes, Barry, your pego confirms the truth of your last remark."

'Well, you don't look a gift horse in the mouth! I covered her lips with my own and instantly we were exchanging the most passionate, burning kiss. Our tongues fluttered in each other's mouths as I raised her dress and petticoats and she arched her back upwards to allow me to pull down her knickers as she tugged down my trousers and drawers to the floor. She continued to rub my cock in her hand as I played with her moistening pussey

15

which was daintily fringed with light brown hair and her cunney lips opened immediately when I inserted my finger between them. We continued to pet and I frigged her juicy cunt with two and then three fingers, faster and faster as I knew that the warm touch of her soft hand would very soon bring me off.

'I could now simply no longer control the tidal flow of jism which was boiling up in my balls. Adrienne sensed that I was about to spend, for with her other hand she quickly pulled down an antimacassar from the top of the sofa and placed the linen cloth on my thighs as she slicked her hand up and down my rigid rod. I began to pant and she felt my cock contract before I squirted my spout of spunk all over her hand. She came too, drenching my fingers with her love juices, but we used her knickers and the antimacassar to wipe up the traces of our escapade before I left shortly afterwards.'

'So you didn't get further than that?' I said, and the disappointment must have shown in my voice for Barry turned round and replied: 'Well, surely you don't think she'd let me fuck her, do you?'

'Why not? You'd be surprised how many girls are just as keen as you on fucking. Don't you listen to anyone who says they don't enjoy it as much as us.'

Barry looked at me and frowned. 'Are you telling me you've already had a woman, young Mountjoy? You lucky so-and-so. I've come pretty close on several occasions and we once employed a Welsh chambermaid named Gladys who sucked me off but I've never actually gone all the way.

Damn it, here am I telling you how to talk to girls and all the time you're way ahead of me!'

'I've just been very lucky,' I replied modestly and I swiftly recounted how I had surrendered my virginity to Diana Wigmore and of my subsequent successes with my pal Frank Folkestone, who Barry had already met at a Liberal Club reception for college freshmen. 'Look, Barry, I know how frustrated you must feel, never having been able to complete the journey, so to speak. Look, I've a splendid idea. Come with me to Doctor Blayers' party tonight. You'll be more than welcome, I'm sure, especially as Frank won't be able to come as he is suffering from a rotten head cold – and you'll make up the numbers.'

At first he demurred. 'That's very kind of you, Rupert, but I just can't barge into a party without being asked. I'm as shy as you when it comes to gate-crashing!'

'Look, if it will make you feel any better I'll ask Jackson to run over with a note to Doctor Blayers asking if you can come in Frank's place.'

He looked gratefully at me. 'Thanks, old boy, I'd much rather go with a proper invite.'

As soon as we arrived back at College I scribbled a quick letter and told the College messenger boy to wait for the reply. Then I strode across to Frank Folkestone's room to see if the poor chap was feeling any better. I didn't knock on the door in case he had fallen asleep and I opened the door very slowly and carefully so as not to disturb him. But though he had earlier told me that he was going to spend the rest of the afternoon trying to sleep off his cold, his bed was

17

empty, though the eiderdown had been thrown back and the bedclothes were ruffled. I was about to leave when suddenly I heard a low moan coming from behind the closed door of his bathroom. Oh dear, I hope Frank isn't feeling really ill, I thought as I marched across the room and flung open the bathroom door with a theatrical flourish.

I needn't have concerned myself! For there was Frank, sitting in the large bath of warm water – not moaning with pain but with passion for with him in the water was Nancy, our young maidservant, who was lathering his erect penis which stood up out of the water like the periscope of a submarine. They were so engrossed in their sexual play that they did not realise that I was there. Nancy got up on her knees and her succulent large breasts jiggled invitingly, which made my balls tingle and my prick stir in my pants. She now rinsed Frank's enormous erection with water and said: 'Now it looks really nice and clean, doesn't it? Let me see if it tastes as good as it looks.'

His eyes closed in ecstacy, Frank leaned back and arched his back up slightly as this time Nancy washed his shiny round knob with her slithering tongue as Frank cupped her big breasts in his hands. Well, the sight of this gorgeous creature holding Frank's shaft whilst she sucked his cock drove me wild and my fingers began to tear wildly at my trouser buttons so that I could release my own stiffstander, which was threatening to burst through the thin material of my flannels. My hand flew to my trusty tool and I wanked away frantically as Nancy now pulled out the plug. As the water level fell, I could see Frank snake out his right arm and plunge his fingers directly into her slippery pussey.

Nancy looked up at me through her half-open eyes which widened to their full extent as she gave a tiny scream. 'Oh, Frank, Frank, someone's come in!'

Frank woke up from his delightful reverie in alarm but as soon as he saw that the uninvited guest who had caught him *in flagrante delicto* was none other than his old chum from St Lionel's his face creased into a grin. 'Not to worry, Nancy, why, it's only Rupert Mountjoy. He and I are best pals and we do everything together. All for one and one for all and all that nonsense.'

She considered this for a moment and said: 'You do, do you? Well, in that case Rupert, why don't you stop rubbing your own cock and let me do it for you once Frank has fucked me with his tremendous tadger?' Here we go again, I thought, for readers of my earlier diaries will note how often I have had to grind my teeth whilst a girl hymns a paean of praise to Frank's gigantic member!

However, I proceeded to shed my clothes whilst Nancy and Frank climbed out of the bath and dried themselves with the huge bathtowels Frank's Mama, Lady Folkestone, had packed for him in his valise when he left home for the Varsity. Nancy and Frank now exchanged a series of slurping kisses and his hands massaged her breasts as her hips swayed in hypnotic rhythm. I cupped my hand over her hairy pussey, rubbing the exposed, erect clitty with my middle finger. But she pushed my hand aside to press in Frank's bulbous bell-end between her cunney lips. She drew about two inches of his thick, meaty shaft inside her cunt and this was enough to drive her insane with desire. Arching her back, she raised herself on tiptoes, forcing more of his prick inside her as she grasped my own iron-hard rod in her right hand.

'I want more of this cock in me – all the way,' she groaned as his fat shaft slid out of her slippery pussey and flopped against her belly. Still holding my cock tightly in her fist, she turned her back to Frank and leaned over the bath, offering her chubby little bottom to him. He parted the peach-like bum cheeks and she turned round and said: 'Frank, don't go up my arse, there's a good boy. I'd be frightened that you'd rend me in two with that mighty tool of yours.'

'Have no fear – I'll only ream out your cunney,' assured Frank as he shoved his truncheon in the inviting cleft between her buttocks and entered her cunt from behind. Nancy pushed her hips back as he plunged his prick all the way into her sopping slit. I watched her hips rotate in a sensuous circular motion as she enjoyed this grand doggie-style fucking. I saw Frank's cock slew in and out of her hot, juicy cunt and Nancy's hand shot up and down my own boner which triggered off my orgasm and my cock unleashed a fountain of sticky white jism that arced across the bath and splashed against the wall. The lewd girl came at the same time as Frank, who sent a gush of warm spunk deep into her cunney, and she came with a full-throated scream of pleasure as her love juices flowed down her thighs.

'How about letting me fuck you now?' I asked

Nancy as, although my cock had lost some of its stiffness, my still enlarged shaft was still swinging heavily between my legs.

'I'd love to, Mister Rupert, but honestly I don't have the time. I'm late as it is and I've still got to clean up the bathroom,' she replied with what appeared to be genuine regret in her voice.

Naturally, after we dressed ourselves we helped Nancy finish her work and I saw Frank slip a sovereign in her hand as she left the room. 'She didn't ask for anything,' he explained as the door closed behind her, 'but yesterday Nancy told me about how she is saving up for a new dress this Christmas and I thought I would help her out.'

'Very generous, I'm sure,' I commented, 'but actually I thought you were down with a bad cold and wouldn't be going to Doctor Blayers' party tonight.'

'I am suffering from a chill though I feel much better after that fuck with Nancy. But I don't think I'll risk going out in the night air, Rupert, if you don't mind. You don't need me to hold your hand there, do you? No, I'll stay in this evening and think of you enjoying yourselves with all those pretty girls.'

'Thank you, Frank, and certainly I don't need you to hold my hand – or anything else for that matter! But I'll certainly be thinking of you wrapped up in bed all on your own.'

Frank flashed a wicked smile. 'Wrapped up, yes but not alone for too long, old boy, for after she's finished her chores, Nancy's promised to tuck me up for the night!'

I rolled my eyes upwards – there had been no

stopping Frank Folkestone ever since Diana and Cecily had first allowed him to cram his cock into their cunnies. 'Bye then, I'll see you tomorrow,' I said as I waved my farewell, thinking that at least Frank's absence might well provide an opportunity for Barry Jacobs to begin his rites of passage.

The messenger returned just as I was about to take a shower to wash away the perspiration from what had just taken place in Frank's bathroom. As expected, Doctor Blayers was disappointed that Frank could not come to his gathering and wished him a speedy recovery, but was delighted that I had procured a substitute at the last minute as he believed in keeping even the numbers of young men and women at his *soirées*. I decided to take down this note to Barry as it would put him at ease, knowing that he would be genuinely welcomed at the reception.

So slipping on a dressing gown, I popped downstairs to his room, and would you believe it, who should be with him when I opened the door which had been left slightly ajar but the voluptuous Nancy. They were entwined together naked on the bed, kissing mouth to mouth as Barry's hand was squeezing her full breasts and she pulled her hand up and down his twitching staff.

'Ahem, we meet again, Nancy,' I said and the shameless minx looked up and grinned saucily, saying: 'Oh fuck, I thought I hadn't closed the door properly. Be a love, Mister Rupert, and shut it firmly behind you.'

I couldn't help laughing as I obeyed her request and I said: 'Do carry on, don't mind me.'

'Fine,' she said, her fist wrapped round Barry's

prick as she moved her hand up and down in regular stroking motions. 'Is that nice, Barry? I'll rub your cock a little harder if you like.'

'Yes please, Nancy, rub a little harder and put your other hand on my balls, move your fingers further back, still further, ahhh, that's wonderful, truly wonderful.' She obliged him and rubbed his shaft at a faster pace until with a hoarse cry he spent, and great globs of frothy, creamy spunk shot out from the top of his purple helmet.

'You're a busy young lady,' I observed as Nancy twisted her body off the bed and bent down to slip on her knickers.

'Yes, there are always a great number of first year students who appreciate my personal services,' she agreed, pulling on her chemise.

'How did you know that I wouldn't have appreciated being asked if I wanted to try out these services?' I wondered.

'Oh, you're on tomorrow's list,' she replied blithely. 'I was going to leave Mister Barry till then but when I came in to empty his wastepaper basket he looked so forlorn I thought I'd see if I could cheer him up a bit, poor boy.'

Barry gave a nervous laugh and added: 'Nancy came in just at the right time to boost my confidence for tonight's affair.'

My eyebrows rose as I exclaimed: 'And I thought that I was the shy fellow. Now I can't even use the gambit of that weird mathematical puzzle you showed me earlier today to open a conversation!'

But before Barry could utter a choice riposte, Nancy sat on the bed and, taking Barry's cock in her hand, said with a puzzled look on her face.

'Do you know, I've only just realised what it is that made Barry's prick look so different to any other tool I've ever handled. What's happened to your foreskin, love – did you have to have it surgically removed? I hope you never caught some kind of nasty disease.'

'No, no, not at all. I've been circumcised, Nancy, and I must say I'm rather surprised that you've never seen a circumcised cock before. Let me explain – circumcision is the biblical covenant God made with Abraham and his descendents, and all Jewish boys have their foreskins removed eight days after birth [or as soon as the infant is deemed medically fit – Editor] by a religious official known as a *mohel*. Muslims too chop off the prepuce for the same religious reason. But quite a few Christian chaps at my school were also circumcised in infancy because a growing number of doctors believe the practice to be hygenic.'

'Yes, there were a few Roundheads in the sixth form at St Lionel's,' I agreed, 'but one poor chap had to undergo the operation when he was fifteen because his foreskin was too tight. It must be a jolly painful operation.'

'For him, maybe,' chuckled Barry, 'but as I was only eight days old when the cut was made, I remember absolutely nothing about it.'

Nancy eyed his circumcised shaft which was beginning to swell up again in her palm. 'Well, you learn something every day. I've never seen one of these shafts before and I must admit that it is not displeasing to the eye. I would imagine that it must feel nice to fuck or to be sucked or tossed off without any additional covering over your cock.

24

'What an awesome and responsible job for the *mohel*,' she added before licking her lips and jamming them over Barry's rubicund mushroom knob and sucking him up to a rock-hard stiffstander.

'It doesn't command any salary as he's expected to donate his fees to charity,' gasped Barry as Nancy's hand cupped his hairy ballsack whilst she continued to lick and lap his pulsating penis which had risen up majestically under her skilful sucking, 'but as any *mohel* will tell you, the wages are poor but the tips are great!'

I smiled my appreciation at this witticism but Nancy was far too involved in palating his prick to have heard his jest. She somehow managed to take almost all of his rampant rod between her lips and bobbed her head up and down so that Barry fucked her mouth without even having to move a muscle! It took less than a minute for Barry's prick to begin to twitch uncontrollably and Nancy's mouth was soon filled with frothy white foam as she swallowed all the jism from his throbbing tool, gulping down every last milky drop of spunk as his shaft shrank back into submission.

'I'm always the best man but never the groom,' I complained as my own prick was now bulging up high against my belly. Nancy flicked open my robe and seeing my raging stiffstander she grinned: 'I'll come round one day soon and we'll see what we can do for Mr John Thomas then.'

There was no time for any further conversation so I went back upstairs to my room and dressed, consoled somewhat by Nancy's promise. By the time Barry and I were ready to go the evening air was rather chill, although a soft light still shone through the windows as we made the short journey across Broad Street to Doctor Blayers' rooms in Jesus College. But when we reached the gates a college servant informed us that the good doctor had booked a hall for his reception at a nearby tavern. At the same time two girls who had also been invited to the party arrived and we escorted them down to a small turning just off Cornmarket Street where the party was taking place. We introduced ourselves as we walked to the new venue and, as always happens in a foursome, we paired off almost immediately. I squired Beth Randall, a charming tall, blonde girl whilst Barry chatted to Esme Dyotte, an equally attractive young lady whose mop of slightly disordered brown hair and dashing hazel eyes spelled out a promise, I thought to myself, of possible further delight later in the evening if my friend played his cards correctly.

Doctor Nicholas Blayers himself welcomed us at the door. He was a jolly, fine-looking man of about forty, edging towards plumpness, sallow complexioned and wearing gold-framed spectacles and a jolly smile. 'Good evening, good evening, how nice to see you!' he beamed as we came in. He had met Beth and Esme before when, at the headmistress' invitation, he had travelled down earlier in the year to lecture to the sixth form at Trippett's Academy. I introduced myself and Barry to him and as the girls turned away temporarily to converse with former schoolfriends who had also won places at Somerville College, Doctor Blayers told us: 'I do hope that you all have an enjoyable evening tonight. You would be surprised at the battles we have had to allow women even to study at the University let alone mix together. Why, many of my own colleagues say to me that the presence of women destroys the atmosphere of Oxford. Only yesterday a certain professor was moaning to me that soon the women will turn round and say: "If we win degrees it is illogical to withold from us the privileges of the High Table." *[The elevated table in the college dining halls at which the principal professors, etc sit – Editor].* To which my reply, of course, is that it would be so much more pleasant to dine in the company of ladies – and this does shock such old dodderers as the gentleman who spoke in such a way to me.

'I believe in the rules of nature and I would like to see young people grow up untrammelled by the burdens of sexual shame. Any tendency of celebration or joy regarding these matters is frowned upon by Society, yet the most elemental expression is itself the act of sexual congress upon which the very preservation of our species is dependent! It is for this reason that Nature made this union extremely pleasurable. We did not ask it; it is the gift of a beneficent Creator and it is thus quite absurd that we are ashamed of our natural inclinations. Do you not agree with me?'

We murmured our assent as we took glasses of iced champagne from a tray proferred to us by a passing waiter and our host continued to ride his hobbyhorse: 'Let me stress that there must be *some* strict regulations by Society – for otherwise we would revert to the laws of the jungle. But in my opinion if two consenting young people wish to follow their natural inclinations, then I say jolly

27

good luck to them – especially if they are responsible enough to take proper care not to bring unwanted children into this overcrowded world.

'Enjoy yourselves tonight,' he added as he turned away to welcome some other guests.

'Gosh, what on earth was that all about?' asked Beth, who only heard the latter part of Doctor Blayers' miniature lecture.

'I believe that he wishes to propound a new morality,' I said, sipping a glass of champagne, to which she gravely nodded and said sweetly: 'Is that so? Personally, I thought he was just expounding upon the joys of fucking.'

I almost choked on my drink as she gave me a saucy smile and murmured throatily: 'Do you like fucking, Rupert? I love it! There is nothing better in the whole wide world I am sure and you don't have to answer the question really because my cousin has already supplied me with your answer!'

'Your cousin? Who is that?'

'Why Diana Wigmore, of course! Yes, she wrote to me about you as soon as she knew that we would both be going up to Oxford together this year. Don't blush, Rupert, she only said nice things about you and your sturdy instrument, which since her tuition you now know how to play to good effect! As soon as you told me your name I thought to myself, it must be fate that has brought us together so quickly.'

Whilst I digested this not unwelcome information, Beth asked: 'Tell me about Barry Jacobs – has he any experience in the art of love-making or like most boys of your years is he still *virgo intacto*?'

'Barry is still untested,' I admitted candidly,

'but I know he is not totally inexperienced and would give anything to enjoy the full delights of l'*amour*.'

'Well, he may well be in luck,' declared Beth, 'for my friend Esme is also possessed of a highly active libido, so let me inform her as to the situation and find out if she also wishes to besport herself tonight. In my opinion Esme will relish the idea of initiating Barry into manhood. Look how well they are getting on together. Oh yes, I am almost certain that your chum will be soon able to divest himself of his tiresome state of virginity.

'It would be rather fun to watch these rites of passage,' she added thoughtfully. 'Do you think your friend would mind forking out for rooms at a local hostelry? An acquaintance of mine in her second year here says that the owner of The Cat and Pigeons, one Mr Thomas Waterbrick, can be trusted to be totally discreet upon payment of a gold sovereign.'

'Barry would gladly take every available room in Mr Waterbrick's hotel in these circumstances,' I laughed.

'Super, that's settled then – I will have words with Esme and confirm that she will be happy to fall in with our plans.'

As Beth had confidently forecast, Esme was more than pleased with our lewd ideas and as for Barry, when I told him how he was about to fuck his first girl, his eyes sparkled and of course he was more than glad to stump up the necessary cash for rooms at The Cat and Pigeons after the party. 'Can we go soon?' he asked eagerly. 'I say old boy, I can't wait to fuck Esme.'

'Steady on, Barry, it would be very rude if we left too early – anyhow, let's get our strength up and tuck into some of that delicious looking food on the buffet table whilst Beth telephones Mr Waterbrick to book our rooms,' I said, though in truth I was also champing at the bit and could hardly wait for the time when I could sweep the soft, willing body of Beth into my arms.

However, the party was most enjoyable and we met some interesting new fellow students as we ate and drank the beautifully prepared refreshments provided. Doctor Blayers was somewhat of a connoisseur of wines and we imbibed perhaps a little too deeply for by the time it was possible to make our farewells, we were all – let us be charitable – quite merry. We hailed a hansom and very soon afterwards found ourselves together in a suite of rooms at The Cat and Pigeons. Beth and I were sitting on the sofa which we had turned round so that we, and Barry and Esme, who when I last actually saw them were sitting on the bed, could enjoy some measure of privacy.

Beth and I cuddled up together and she began to arouse me by resting her hand on my penis. Our heads turned towards each other and inexorably our lips moved forwards to meet and we exchanged the most passionate of kisses. As we embraced she began to massage my prick gently and naturally it responded by swelling up and becoming harder and harder under her touch.

Somehow the fact that Barry and Esme were behind us whilst Beth was fiddling with my fly buttons did not inhibit me in the slightest. In fact, to be honest their presence seemed to have the opposite effect and frankly it excited me to think that they might be watching as I took the initiative and unbuttoned Beth's blouse and slid my hand over her rounded bosoms. Now perhaps our exhibition had encouraged them because when she brought my stiff shaft out into the open I heard a gasp behind me and I surmised that Barry and Esme had begun their own sex play. I probed the inside of Beth's mouth with my tongue and slid down the straps of her chemise over her shoulders to expose her proud, jutting breasts. She closed her fingers around my palpitating pillar and began to toss me off with regular stroking motions which sent tiny shivers of pleasure all over my body.

Behind us I could hear that Barry and Esme were already one step ahead as I could distinctly hear the wet, squishy sounds of Esme's pussey being finger-fucked, and her moans of delight stimulated Beth who pulled her dress and petticoat up to her waist, exposing her frilly French knickers. She arched her back to assist me in removing them and she spread her legs as I let my palm smooth its way into her silky pubic thatch. My fingers easily found her moist crack and I slowly stroked the entire length of her slit before dipping my finger into her wet cunney, which sent her wild, and she twisted and turned as I moved first one and then two fingers in and out of her dripping cunt.

I turned my head to watch Barry performing the same service for Esme and then Beth pulled down my trousers and drawers and in a flash her head was between my legs as, shaking a lock of blonde hair from her face, she took my shiny uncapped helmet into her mouth. She sucked slowly, tickling and working round the little 'eye' on top of the bulbous dome. Her magic tongue encircled my helmet, savouring its spongy texture and her teeth scraped the tender flesh so deliciously as she drew me in between those luscious lips. She lowered her head to take in more of my shaft and ran her tongue along the side of my throbbing tool which again sent almost unbearable waves of sheer ecstacy coursing through my entire frame. Every time she sensed I was on the verge of spending she would ease her wicked tonguing, thus prolonging our mutual enjoyment which was reaching new, unscaled heights of desire.

'You'll come too quickly if I don't stop for a while' Beth whispered as she reached round and unfastened the hook of her dress, leaving me to unbutton the garment. She slid gracefully out of it and I drank in the awesome beauty of her glorious naked body. Her bare breasts rose and fell with her heavy breathing and until my dying hour I will never forget the sight of the firm swell of those proud young beauties, perhaps the most perfect I have ever viewed. They were firm and globular, each looking slightly away from each other and tapering into lovely curves until they came to the rich, crimson points of her taut nipples.

I kissed and sucked these pretty, erect titties and she took my stiffstander in her fist for a second time but now she lay back and held my pulsating prick against her warm, white belly. I moved to insert my knob between Beth's inviting cunney lips but instead she pulled my cock forwards into the cleft between those divinely rounded breasts and rubbed my cock between the exquisitely formed globes whilst she cupped my ballsack in one hand and frigged her own pussey with the other. It was impossible to hold back and I spurted my spunk all over her bosoms. She let go of my shaft to rub the hot, sticky cream all over her titties until I had emptied my balls and my staff began to flag, settling down in a semi-erect state, between her breasts.

In our frenzy we had taken no notice of what was happening behind us, but now as we were in a more composed state, we looked back to see what stage of the game Barry and Esme had reached. It was immediately apparent that they were not far behind us as both had shed their clothes and Esme was kissing Barry's thick prick which was quivering in anticipation. Her tongue encircled his knob, savouring a blob of pre-spend juice which had already formed there as she drew him in between her generous red lips, sucking lustily. Barry instinctively pushed upwards as her warm hands played with his heavy, hanging balls and her pliant tongue washed over the purple mushroom of his helmet.

'A-h-r-e, A-h-r-e!' he growled softly as Esme took her lips away from his prick and lay back, her legs wide apart to give us all a full view of her curly moss of cunney hair and the pouting pussey lips and delicious red love chink. She took his cock in her hand to press the glowing head between the soft moist cunney lips and I thought to myself, here you go, old boy, your cock is about to enter a cunt for the first time and experience those grand thrills which only a good fuck can induce.

But then disaster struck! Poor Barry's prick,

which before was as hard as an iron bar, appeared to bend as he frantically rubbed his knob against Esme's juicy cunney lips. Indeed, the harder he rubbed his rod against her sopping slit, the softer it became until it lay as limp as could be in her pussey hair. Beads of perspiration were now evident on his forehead as he cried out in frustration: 'What the hell is happening to my cock? I've waited years for this and now it's letting me down!'

'Calm down, it isn't unusual for a lad about to fuck for the first time to be so nervous that his prick won't stand up,' Beth assured him. 'Look, watch Rupert fuck me and I'll wager you'll be ready to play a tune on your organ in no time at all.'

Barry was not to be consoled as in vain he frantically attempted to frig his recalcitrant cock up to its former erection. 'It won't go up, it just won't go up. Oh Esme, I am so sorry – what you must think of me!' he groaned as he slid his hand up and down his dangling dick.

'You silly boy, you must try not to think about it, and I guarantee that Mother Nature will take its course,' said Esme soothingly. 'And before you say anything more, you have no need to fret about my feelings as I always enjoy watching a good fuck. It makes me very horny too and we'll enjoy ourselves that much more afterwards.'

I don't know whether Barry was entirely convinced but naturally I was more than ready to help out my friend by fucking the beautiful Beth, who said: 'Move up you two lovebirds, Rupert and I will join you on the bed and you will both have a grandstand view of his cock entering my cunt.'

We embraced as we rolled together on the bed next to the other pair and as we writhed about in each other's arms my prick began to leap and dance about between her thighs, seeking an entrance in the silky mass of blonde pussey hair which formed a perfect veil over her pouting pussey. I wanted to fuck the sweet girl then and there but I knew that I had to instruct Barry in how to approach a cunt with subtlety. So I disengaged my mouth from Beth's burning kiss and rose up on my knees between her parted legs. My hands roved around her gorgeous breasts and I fingered the engorged, rubbery nipples that stood out like little red soldiers. I heard her gasp with joy as I buried my face in the golden fleece of her pubic bush, inhaling the delicate aroma of her cunt. I grasped her bum cheeks as I flicked my tongue around her crack and she whimpered as her pussey opened like a budding flower and I slipped the tip of my tongue inside her love lips to probe against her stiffening clitty. I licked and lapped as her cunney gushed love juice and her body rocked with unslaked desire.

'Fuck me, Rupert, fuck me,' she moaned and so I scrambled up to kneel between her marble white legs as she reached out and clasped her hand round my swollen shaft.

'I hope you're watching very carefully, Barry,' I said as Beth guided my cock into her dripping love channel. Ah, to hold her creamy buttocks was sheer delight and to suck her erect rosy titties was heaven itself as I slid my cock in and out of her warm, clinging cunney.

Our movements became more heated as I

thrust forward, sending my prick deep inside her. How I enjoyed this magnificent fuck, sliding my willing cock in and out of her wet and juicy pussey. Beth yelped as she felt my knob touch the innermost walls of her cunt and she wrapped her legs around my waist to hold me firmly inside her as I continued to pound away, my prick driving in and out of the tender folds of her cunney from which her juices were flowing liberally. Then she started to buck to and fro with her bum cheeks lifting themselves off the sheets and I pumped into her back and forth as her body gyrated wildly. I felt her body tremble as she closed her legs around me like a vice.

'Yes . . . yes . . . I'm coming . . . yes, yes, Oooh! Oooh! Ah!' Beth yelled as she shuddered her way to a delicious spend. When she had calmed down I set up another rhythm, fucking her with short, sharp jabs and she spent again as I warned her that my own spend was near. She massaged the underside of my ballsack and this brought on my final surge as I emptied myself into her, flooding her cunney with tremendous spurts of hot, sticky spunk and she screamed with delight as the gush of my juices sent shock after shock of erotic energy coursing through our veins.

I heaved myself off Beth and we turned ourselves to our right to see that, as we had expected, the sensual spectacle of our fucking had achieved the desired effect and that Barry's battering ram was impatiently pushing its way through Esme's curly forest of cunney hair. However, his inexperience showed as he was unable to find his way through the hirsute veil to her cunt, so I said to him: 'Wait a second, Barry, let me help you.' I inserted my hand between their bellies and told Barry to lift himself up for a moment. Then I took hold of Barry's rock-hard cock and directed the fiery knob towards Esme's pouting pussey lips. 'Now slide your prick forward and you will see that the key will fit into the lock,' I ordered as I took my hand away, and with his first thrust he was within the lips, with the second he was half way home and with the third his entire pulsating shaft was firmly ensconced inside her wet, willing honeypot.

Barry's body trembled with excitement and his tight little arse cheeks quivered. As Beth and I noted with satisfaction, Barry had a natural understanding of what was required of him and he refrained from rushing in and out of Esme's juicy cunney in a mad frenzy but instead forced himself to push in and out as slowly as he could. This was most pleasing to Esme who responded with upward heaves to his downward thrusts. Her bottom rolled violently as she clawed Barry's back and he grasped her shoulders and started to ride her like a cowboy with a bucking bronco. Her legs slid down, her heels drumming against the mattress as she arched her back, working her love channel back and forth against the hot, velvety hardness of Barry's thick, glistening tool.

With a hoarse cry of rapture he sheathed his shaft so fully within her that his balls nestled against the top of her thighs. This so affected Esme that she rotated her hips wildly, lifting her lovely bottom to obtain the maximum contact with his cock. He groaned as Esme's fingernails raked across his back and she panted: 'Oh lovely, that's really lovely, Barry, ah, it's so delicious! Make me come now, you big cocked boy! Shoot your spunk into me!' She threw back her head in abandon and a primordial sound came from deep within her as her climax spilled out and she swam in her sea of voluptuous delight just as Barry shuddered convulsively as he squirted his tribute of frothy white jism into her yearning cunney, on and on until the last faint dribblings oozed out and he sank down upon her in a blissful swoon of unalloyed happiness.

My own cock was now standing as straight and erect as before and Beth could see that I was game for another bout, but the unselfish girl turned to her friend and invited her to make use of my pulsating prick. 'Thank you, my sweet,' said Esme, smiling lasciviously at me. 'My cunt is a little sore from Barry's big cock but I would love to suck this fine-looking cock, if its owner has no objection.'

'None at all, please help yourself,' I said as I wriggled my way towards her until she could pull my aching shaft towards her rich red lips. She squirmed towards me to leave Barry lying on his own as she took my knob inside her mouth and washed it all over with her tongue, making me shudder all over. She quickened the movements of her tongue, lashing away at my rigid rod as her right hand snaked down and frigged busily away at her still juicy cunt. Esme's mouth was like a cavern of fire which warmed yet did not burn as she licked and lapped away, stroking her tongue up and down the sensitive underside which made me almost faint away with the pleasure of it all.

Then she cupped her hands around my balls, gently rubbing them as she slowly took every inch of my prick into her mouth. She squeezed her free hand around the base of my cock, sucking me harder and harder until I felt the tingling sensation which heralded the nearness of my spend. I shouted that I was going to spunk very soon and the randy girl let my twitching tadger slide out of her mouth.

For a moment I thought this was simply because she did not want to swallow my sperm and would simply finish me off with her hand. But I was wrong for she cried: 'Pump into my cunt!' So I slid myself down her trembling body, ramming my prick into her soaking pussey which was still wet from Barry's and her own juices, but she waggled her bum so artfully that her cunney muscles gripped my cock wonderfully as I drew my chopper out and then darted it in again to engorge this marvellous cunney, which held my thick prick like a soft, moist hand. To be absolutely truthful, as I must in these memoirs, Esme was an even better fuck than Beth for she expert in the use of her vaginal muscles to contract and relax her cunney, and she somehow managed to tighten her passage so when I slowly drew out my gleaming shaft until only the tip of the purple dome remained embedded inside her, it caused so great a suction that it sent electric shocks of delight fizzling through me. I worked away for as long as I could hold back and she spent twice until the sensitive contractions of her clever little love channel milked my cock of a torrent of hot, sticky cream that lubricated her innermost passages.

The sight of this sensual show had so stimulated Beth that when I recovered my composure I turned my head to see her lying on her back with her legs apart, her hands provocatively rubbing her blonde muff. 'Go on, Barry Jacobs, what are you waiting for?' cried Esme, pushing him towards the other girl. Their bodies met and Barry slid his hand over her dripping pussey, then he spread open her cunney lips and she purred happily as he rhythmically finger-fucked her.

'Have you ever eaten pussey?' Esme demanded and Barry looked up and shook his head.

'Watch closely and I'll show you how to do it,' I said and I doved down into Beth's blonde bush, rubbing my face against her silky golden hair. Barry withdrew his fingers as I worked my tongue along that delicate crack. My mouth was now put to good use as it slid up and down the warm slit and I savoured the tangy taste of drops of love juice which pattered down from her cunney. I heard Beth gasp with pleasure as I probed her love lips and thrust my tongue deep into her cunt, finding her erect clitty and sucking it into my mouth as she moaned with pleasure and brought herself off by rubbing her cunt against my mouth. Almost of their own volition her legs splayed wider as she sought to open herself still more to me. I slurped lustily, swallowing her salty libation that was flowing freely from her pussey and Beth's hands held my head as her legs, now folded across my shoulders, twitched convulsively with joy as the waves of pleasure from her spend engulfed her.

'Somebody fuck me please,' she called out and

my head jerked up from between her thighs as Barry's circumcised cock passed inches away from my face on its way to the slippery entrance which was waiting to welcome it. I could see my friend's whole being was shaking with excitement as the swollen helmet of his rock-hard rod teased Beth's pussey lips before he edged his shaft deep inside her juice-wet love furrow. His hands roved around her jutting breasts, arousing the rosy nipples until they stuck out proudly, as he began to fuck her at first slowly but then increasing the speed of his strokes until his prick was hammering like a piston, his balls beating a tattoo against her backside. Barry showed that he was an ardent cocksman but all too soon he felt himself approach the ultimate pleasure stroke.

'I'm coming! I'm coming! I can't stop!' he shrieked as his body exploded into a climactic release and he shot his hot, creamy froth into Beth's delicious cunt as she writhed beneath him, lifting her shapely bum cheeks to obtain the maximum contact with his raging cock.

We were not yet sated, dear reader. As I lay flat on my back, my love truncheon standing as high and straight as a flagpole, Esme struggled up and stood over me, her legs apart like a female Colossus. Her teeth flashed in a lustful smile, her hazel eyes twinkled merrily and then, holding her cunney lips open with her hands, she slowly lowered herself onto me. As she went down on me, my greased shaft slid straight into her at the first attempt and our pubic bones ground together. She paused, like a rider testing a new mount, clamping her cunney muscles around my penis as I flexed myself, heaving myself upwards and delighting in the silky clinginess of her cunt which fitted my cock like a hand-made glove.

Esme pumped her tight little bottom up and down, digging her fingernails into my flesh, and each voluptuous shove was accompanied by wails of ecstacy. I pulled her body forward so as I could rub her red titties between my fingers and then I moved my head up to take one of the stiff little strawberries between my lips. She panted away as she bounced up and down on my pulsing prick so violently that I was forced to hold her bum cheeks to keep her in position, helping her in her ride by pushing her up and letting her drop down hard upon my cock. The supreme moment arrived and her cunney clung to my cock even harder as she pulled me in as firmly as she could, squeezing her legs against mine as if fearing that I would leave her. She sighed and squirmed, the lips of her cunt tightly clipping my shaft as we spent profusely together, my jets of sperm spurting up her pussey as her own love juices cascaded down her thighs. Her buttocks quivered in my hands as we drained each other dry until Esme slowed her movements down and came finally to rest. We lay entwined in euphoric peace and she exclaimed in a tone of rapture: 'Oh, that was a truly magnificent fuck, Rupert. I must award your cock full marks for his performance. You know, Beth, it has to be said that boys are adept and considerate lovers. We have chosen our bedmates well tonight.'

'Let me say that the feeling is mutual,' Barry said, his voice cracking with emotion. 'I will never forget either of you helping me so patiently to lose my cherry. I count myself most fortunate in making love for the first time with two such understanding girls.'

Beth acknowledged the compliment and said: 'Perhaps we should all drink a toast to Dame Agatha Humphrey of St Trippett's Academy for The Daughters of Gentlefolk. Unlike the vast majority of schools, we were given guidance on sexual matters.'

'Yes, I can remember telling Dame Agatha without any embarrassment of my first sensual stirrings,' Esme chipped in brightly. 'I had been waking up in the night and finding myself shivering with excitement, with my nightdress damp from a thin fluid which had trickled down my thighs from my then lightly haired pussey. Now I knew from other girls who I had seen giggling over the pages of that rude magazine *The Oyster* that boys entering puberty have nocturnal emissions but I never knew that girls could have wet dreams.

'Golly, I was so worried and confused but in the end I plucked up courage and asked Dame Agatha about what was happening to my body and she told me how entirely normal these nightly emissions were and how my body was preparing itself for sexual congress.'

'Not that we were totally innocent about sex by the time we had the first hairs growing around our pussies,' said Beth brightly.

'Did you play games in the dormitories like we used to do?' I asked her.

'Of course, although we made ourselves follow to the letter some strict regulations about such matters,' she rejoined, passing a glass of wine to me. 'Perhaps the most charming rule concerned the bathrooms in the evenings as we prepared ourselves for bed. Naturally, shut up as we were with little chance of contact with the opposite sex, passions and crushes freely abounded. Many a swift hip-to-hip rub was exchanged as a signal that greater intimacies might be enjoyed in the near future. But to counter the shame and embarrassment of rejection we all accepted the convention that if the girl you fancied was bending over a washbasin having her before lights-out wash, it was totally permissible to approach her from behind and to touch and stroke her – mark you, without a word being uttered. If she did not check these advances it was permissible to reach under her nightie and clasp the swelling cheeks of her bum. Then, so long as she continued to show no objection, one might rub one's pussey against her bottom and then reach round and play with her hairy bush, though more than a little diddling was frowned upon as it might upset other would-be suitors. A caress of one's cunney held the promise of fun and games between the sheets later that night.'

'But wasn't it rather difficult for anyone to repel such an advance?' enquired Barry.

'Not really, for one could easily reach back with one's hand and remove the persistent hand. There are many subtle ways by which one can quietly yet firmly refuse unwelcome attentions and I think that Esme will agree that women are far more skilled than men in expressing themselves in this unspoken language.'

Esme nodded her head in agreement. 'It was also so nice to be able to use this very delicate way of accepting a loving, exploratory caress. My goodness, when I think back how many times whilst splashing water over my face I sensed a warm presence behind me and felt the soft touch of an unknown hand running up and down my back and sliding under my nightie to squeeze my bottom. It was such fun to close your eyes, cradling your head on your arms against the cold rim of the wash-basin, nestling against the unseen girl whose hands would reach round and cup your breasts in her palms, rubbing up the titties until they rose up to greet her.

'Yes, and how stimulating it could be to feel a quiver of delight run through the body of the girl you were stroking, to look in the mirror and see her blush as she shyly raised her bum to show that she welcomed your attention. Then would come the magic moment when you raised the nightdress over the hips and the white orbs of her bottom were exposed to be cupped, caressed or even lightly slapped. And ah, the delight if afterwards she welcomed the insertion of your finger into the dampness of her cunney, wriggling so sweetly as you prised open the yielding love lips.

'Beth and I often used this stratagem before starting to play games in bed, though perhaps we should not mention such sport to you,' added Esme with a saucy look.

'Oh, please go on, Esme, don't be a tease,' begged Barry. 'Rupert and I would really love to hear all about what you got up to together, wouldn't we, old chap?'

Before I could answer (in the affirmative, of course!), Beth interrupted and said: 'All right, we'll tell you all but you must confess your early experiences to us afterwards.'

This was a fair enough exchange so we agreed and settled down to listen to Esme, but she had little to say except that 'actions spoke louder than words' and so she and Beth would demonstrate what they often did, cuddled together in bed at St Trippett's, and this proved to be so exciting that Barry and I never got round to fulfilling our side of the bargain!

Barry and I settled down to watch as the two girls entwined their arms lasciviously around each other. I looked again at Beth and how magnificent her breasts looked, rounded like two snowy white balloons topped with two cute, rosy nipples. She squeezed her legs tightly together and her right hand went down to snake its path through the golden silk of her blonde mound. She started to rub it gently with the palm of her hand and to move her backside slowly, lazily dipping her fingertip into her itching cunney. Esme now knelt beside her, stroking and fondling Beth's nipples as she removed the blonde girl's hand and replaced it with her own, inserting two fingers into her sticky pussey, jerking them in and out, whilst her thumb brushed over the erect clitty which protruded between Beth's cunney lips.

This was but the *hors d'oeuvre* to the main course of a girls-only fuck because she rolled herself on top of Beth, taking care that her hand did not lose contact with the juicy love nest which was becoming more moist by the minute. Her apt fingers toyed with Beth's erect clitty as Esme breathed: 'What a gorgeous wet cunt you have, darling. Can you feel my fingers dipping in and out of your honeypot? Does that feel good – or would you prefer a big fat cock like Rupert's piercing you through and through?'

Beth moaned an inaudible reply as Esme now kissed the damp yellow pussey hair around the cunney lips and her pretty pointed tongue licked lewdly along Beth's crack. She soon found her clitty, fully swollen as she sucked the little button, letting the very tip of her long tongue go around it in tiny circles. Barry and I craned our heads forward to watch her teeth nibble all along the glorious love slit, her pink tongue teasing Beth's tasty pussey with rasping licks.

'Oh! Oh!' Beth gasped, her eyes closed in heavenly bliss and she took hold of Esme's tousled head in her hands. 'Oh, you tongue me so divinely, darling.' Her soft limbs quivered as Esme pressed her face even harder against Beth's cunney lips so that her tongue could delve even deeper and she lapped around the innermost walls of the orifice. Beth writhed around in frenzied momentum as Esme's tongue, now glued to her cunney lips, worked sensuously inside the hole to be rewarded by a sustained flow of pungent love juice which she swallowed as Beth worked herself off with wild, rising cries of joy.

Now it was Beth's turn to be the gentleman and she rolled off the bed and padded across to the table on which stood the tray of refreshments we had ordered. She brought back an empty bottle of champagne with her and then she took out a small jar of cold cream from her handbag. Barry and I looked on curiously as she turned Esme gently on to her side. Beth's ideas for pleasuring the other girl soon became apparent as she rubbed the cream in and around Esme's wrinkled little bum hole, and the auburn-haired beauty wriggled deliciously, her smooth white globes jiggling as Beth lubricated her rear dimple. Then Beth took the champagne bottle and with great care slid the neck, which was as thick as my prick, into Esme's behind. The girl gave a cry of alarm but then her pretty face relaxed, the hazel eyes wide and appealing as Beth now began work in earnest. With one hand she manipulated Esme's sensitive cunney lips and clitty and with the other she moved the neck of the bottle back and forth gently in and out of Esme's anus.

'Aaaah! Aaaah! Aaaah!' she cried out as Beth continued this inexorable masturbation. 'Oh Beth, you are a naughty girl to fuck my cunney and bum at the same time. All I need is a thick cock in my mouth and I will be filled to the brim. Where are you, Barry, I need you!'

This was all he had to hear – for like me, Barry's prick was now standing high against his belly and he shuffled forward, his prick in his hand, and to his delight Esme grabbed hold of it and her mouth opened greedily over his knob as she took it between her lips, slurping lustily on the shaft, sending him into paroxyms of delight. I could no longer stand idly by and I crawled round behind Beth and parted her peach bottom cheeks and inserted two or three inches of my bursting prick into her damp cunt from behind. She turned her head so that our lips could meet and she drew my tongue into her mouth as she cleverly wriggled her bum so that I could embed my entire eight and a half inches of cock inside her. With a passionate jolt of our loins my shaft was fully inserted and she cried out in glee as I started to fuck her and our hips began to work away in unison. How tightly her dripping cunt enclasped my cock and we gloried with each tremendous thrust as her juices dripped upon my balls as they slapped against her arse.

She threw back her head in ecstacy, tossing her blonde mane over her shoulders as she urged me to drive even deeper and with her firm bottom cheeks cupped in my broad palms, she writhed savagely whilst my sinewy shaft rammed its passage in and out of her soaking slit. I could feel the throbbing of Beth's excited pussey increase to boiling point as she screamed out her climax so loudly that I feared we might disturb other guests in the hotel. Her shuddering cries soon led to my twitching cock ejaculating great gushes of jism inside her cunney just as her orgasm was dying down, giving the sensual lady the pleasure of a second spend which arose from the sensation of my spunk hurtling into her love channel. Now Barry could contain himself no longer and he thrust his hips forward and his sperm spurted into Esme's waiting throat. She tried hard to swallow all of the creamy emission but he shot such a torrent between her lips that some of the fluid dripped down her chin and onto her breasts.

This led to Beth increasing the speed of her finger-fucking of Esme's pussey and together with continued insertion of the champagne bottle up her bum soon brought off the sweet girl to a magnificent orgasm.

This last 'whoresome foursome', as my first lovely partner-in-fucking Diana Wigmore was wont to call such jousts, completely exhausted us and we all fell fast asleep under the warm eiderdown Beth and I pulled across the bed. Our tangled limbs rested in comfort until the grey dawn of morning woke me from my slumber. The others still lay deep in the arms of Morpheus when as quietly as possible, I slid out of bed and padded to the bathroom to make my ablutions.

Ah, what sweet recollections this memoir brings back to me, of how Beth, Esme and Barry lay naked on crushed and rumpled sheets whilst I watched the weak autumn sunlight caress the dreaming spires as the town woke up to another day. I looked out at the early risers walking down the street and I idly wondered how many of them had enjoyed as good a fucking (if at all) as Barry and I.

An attractive dark-haired girl in jodhpurs strode towards the Bodleian Library [one of the most famous libraries in the world with an unrivalled collection of rare books and manuscripts – Editor] and two or three male passers-by turned their heads to stare after her. I pondered as to what private thoughts were passing through her mind and those of her unknown secret admirers. What ideas were spinning around those people, hiding behind bland, expressionless faces, what lovers, real and imaginary were being wooed in their minds, what triumphs and failures were being lived and relived in their daydreams? Take this girl who turned heads on this October morning, for instance; what were the thoughts of the young butcher's boy who was so entranced by the fetching swell of the girl's buttocks tightly encased in the riding breeches which clung so lovingly to her figure, that he pulled his bicycle over to the kerb so he could gaze at the girl's delicious backside for a few moments more? Perhaps he was thinking of how he would like to see her peel off her clinging jodhpurs and expose her naked charms or maybe how she might caress his erect cock or even be persuaded to take his knob in her mouth?

It is this gap between reality and fantasy, between what is and what might be or might have been which has for me been an endless source of fascination. Will the fucking of a particular girl turn out to be an anticlimax? Will the reality be but a pale imitation of the untrammelled adventures of the mind? Fantasy should not be discouraged for it represents perhaps the only time when one can be certain of taking the lead role in delicious daydreams in which one can become famous for whatever one wishes. All grievances can be righted, all one's actions will be applauded and, of course, a variety of the most gorgeous women in the entire world will be conquered almost without effort! Curmudgeonly critics may carp at fantasising as a fruitless exercise – but surely the only harm in pursuing this occupation is when one finds it difficult to leave cloud-cuckoo land for the harsher world of reality upon which we have so little chance to influence the way events great and small unfold around us.

The rays of the sun roused me from this reverie and I turned back to see that my companions were still asleep. But Beth lay on her back, her nude charms half uncovered by the bed-clothes which sent my prick rearing up to a fine hard stiffness. I gently climbed between her open legs and kissed her blonde furry pussey. Then I spread the pouting cunney lips with one hand and taking hold of my cock with the other, I lowered my uncapped helmet until it touched her pouting cunney lips. I managed to insinuate my knob inside her cunt without waking her. She made a few uneasy movements as I slowly withdrew my blue-veined pole but Beth slept on as this time I engulfed my staff fully into her love channel, overcome as she was by the fatigues of fucking the previous night. I would have liked to continue this delicate fuck but alas, *tempus fugit*, and I had to leave shortly to attend a lecture in political philosophy. So I was forced to begin heaving and bucking in earnest and this woke the pretty girl, who fondly kissed me, and we engaged in a wonderful contest, each striving to be first in climbing the mountain to the highest peak of pleasure. My thrusts forward were met with her impetuous heaves upwards and as my shaft slid to the hairs inside her honeypot my balls knocked against Beth's thighs and the delicious wriggles of her splendid bottom soon roused me to an erotic fury.

Our frenzied fucking woke Barry and Esme and

they immediately copied our example. It was so arousing to see Esme's beautiful cleft in its hairy auburn grotto with the large white shaft of Barry's weapon appearing and disappearing through the luxuriant curly thatch of pussey hair as he drove his cock in and out of the open, rosy chink. Our frantic heaves and shoves were received and returned by our lusty partners with a gradually increasing intensity until we all four spent near enough simultaneously, swimming in a sea of lubricity as we melted away in a glorious excess of sensual rapture.

We lay there for a while longer but then it was time to wash and dress and we ate a hearty breakfast. Barry paid the bill and we made arrangements to meet the girls again in a few days' time. 'Will you get into trouble for staying out all night?' I asked, much concerned that this escapade would have no serious consequences for the two lovely ladies.

'No, Mr Holland the porter is very obliging and a half sovereign will buy his silence,' said Esme with a giggle as we exchanged fond kisses of farewell. 'How do you boys plan to get back into your rooms?' Barry explained that we hoped to enter our college through a secret back entrance our maidservant Nancy had shown us (we didn't venture any further information about the other services Nancy provided for her scholars!) and we waved goodbye as we walked through town.

By taking the seldom-used side stairs that Nancy had pointed out, we managed to sneak into our college unnoticed and I hastily changed and ran down the stairs to the lecture hall just in time to take my place before our senior lecturer, Professor Simon 'Beaver' Webb, entered the room. He was a large, indeed somewhat corpulent gentleman with twinkling blue eyes and a luxuriant red beard which doubtless accounted for his admittedly vulgar nickname. An ardent supporter of the suffragettes, his radical views were hardly hidden in his dissertation on the so-called 'wild women' who were determined to change the country's social structure.

But frankly, I was so tired after all the exertions of the previous night that my eyes fluttered shut more than once whilst the Professor gave us his views on why women should be allowed to vote. However, he became quite steamed up at the end of his lecture and I woke up with a start as he thundered: 'We must allow for the fact that there is no reason to suppose that in any respect women will show themselves superior in sagacity. Blunders will undoubtedly result occasionally from the new freedom when it finally arrives – and I say "when" and not "if" advisedly for the river of social progress can only be stemmed, it can never be rolled back. And if the new movement has no other effect than to rouse women to rebellion against the madness of producing large families, it would confer a priceless blessing on themselves and upon humanity!'

A burst of applause came from a small group of girls from Girton College, Cambridge who had been specially invited with other students from London and Edinburgh to attend a special three day seminar presided over by Professor Webb on

'The Emancipation Of Women'. Not all the undergraduates agreed with the Professor's sentiments however, and a few ill-mannered boors had the temerity to hiss as Professor Webb gathered up his papers.

At first I thought the Professor was going to ignore the jeers but he changed his mind as he reached the door and he suddenly whirled round and accosted Lord Blaxonberry who had led the dissenters. 'So you and your friends do not approve of votes for women,' he snapped angrily. 'Perhaps you do not approve of votes for men either.'

'Not particularly,' the wealthy young landowner coolly replied. 'I would have to agree with you that the prevailing democratic tendency is the prevailing fashionable theory. The idea of government by the absolute majority has superseded the thought that government should be conducted for the benefit of all by the enlightened and capable – the genuine aristocracy in the strict sense of the word – who have been born and bred to such a task.

'In my view, Professor, the only benefit of granting women the franchise might be to show the innate fallacies inherent in the pernicious democratic doctrine and weaken the belief in the wisdom of purely popular government.'

'Stuff and nonsense!' called out a very pretty girl from just a few seats away from me. 'I would rather be governed by a council of working men who know at first hand the needs of the great majority of our citizens than a gathering of chinless drones who know nothing except how to idle away their days whilst the rest of their fellow countrymen engage in back-breaking toil.'

'Hear, hear! Well said!' I cried out loudly, and this interjection brought me a friendly smile from the speaker and a disdainful look of utter contempt from Lord Blaxonberry.

Professor Webb stroked his luxuriant red beard and said: 'Carry on, sir. What would you add to this discussion?'

I thought carefully before rising to reply. 'I would just wish to add this thought, sir,' I said, trying as hard as possible to prevent my knees from shaking, as public speaking has always filled me with dread and was one of the major reasons why I recently refused the kind offer of Mr Lloyd George to stand as the Liberal parliamentary candidate in the safe seat of West Gloucestershire during the recent General Election. 'There is no sadder sight in the world than that of a wasted life, yet how wantonly Society condemns to waste the lives of thousands upon thousands of bright, intelligent young women all over Britain whose powers are worn down and diminished by long courses of boring trivialities and mental stagnation.'

Though I stand in danger of being labelled a braggart, I can truthfully record that my words were cheered to the echo, not least by the attractive girl whose own speech had sparked off my contribution. Professor Webb brought the discussion to a close and enjoined us to read a variety of books on female emancipation – both for and against – and told us to write essays upon the subject that he wanted handed in to him in three weeks' time.

As we left the lecture hall, I smiled back at the

girl whose cause I had supported and she made her way round to my desk and introduced herself. 'My name is Gillian Headleigh from Girton College, Cambridge and I'm the secretary of the college branch of the Cambridge Society For Women's Rights,' she said, holding out her hand. 'Thank you very much for supporting me against Lord Blaxonberry and his little coterie of silly young reactionary idiots.'

'I'm Rupert Mountjoy and I'm studying here at Balliol,' I said, shaking her proferred hand. 'The authorities here are usually so stuffy about male and female undergraduates mixing together that I'm surprised you managed to obtain a pass to listen to Professor Webb's lecture.'

She laughed and though we were talking of serious matters I could not help but be diverted by her mop of bright curls that set off her tiny, slightly *retroussé* nose and large cornflower-blue eyes which sparkled with promise. Her slim, lithe body was delightfully shown off by a close-fitting grey costume in the modern style, which accentuated the swell of her small but gorgeously rounded breasts that jutted proudly forward like two soft peaches ripe for my mouth . . .

'Doctor Blayers arranged it for a group of us to come over to Oxford and attend a number of lectures as part of our PPE [*Politics, Philosophy and Economics — Editor*] course. There are many excellent scholars at Cambridge but it is generally agreed that Professor Webb [*a distant relative of the well-known social reformers and educationalists Beatrice and Sidney Webb who helped found the London School of Economics in 1895 — Editor*] is the most important figure in the drive towards social progress.'

'What a coincidence,' I exclaimed. 'I was at a party given by Doctor Blayers last night.'

'Yes, I was there too and I saw you talking to a pretty blonde girl,' she said with a little smile which showed two delicious dimples on either side of her lovely red lips.

'Would you like to take morning coffee with me?' I asked hurriedly, for I had no desire to let the conversation drift down this particular avenue! Gillian agreed and fortunately I had no further lectures until mid-afternoon so after coffee I was able to walk down with her to her lodgings in Pusey Street, just off the Woodstock Road. We chatted in animated fashion and by the time we reached the house in which Gillian and three other girls were staying for the week, almost to my surprise, I noticed that we were holding hands.

'I have some reading to catch up on,' she said, 'but you're welcome to join me if you are free.' I accepted this invitation with alacrity for the sun had come out and the weather was warm enough to sit outside, which I thought would be especially pleasant as the other girls were studying elsewhere and so we had the house to ourselves. I pulled out a rug and two deckchairs from the garden shed but Gillian sat herself down on the rug and of course I followed suit.

At first we both attempted to read but when I put my book down and took the trembling girl in my arms she did not push me away but giggled delightfully and brought her face up to be kissed. Our mouths met and in an instant her tongue was filling my mouth, probing, lapping and caressing, which made my prick swell up to its full height. My fingers found their way to the buttons of her blouse and I undid enough of them to allow me to slip my hand inside and squeeze the succulent spheres of her breasts, feeling the hardening nipples push against my palm. My excited prick was now threatening to burst its way out from the confines of my trousers but she slid her hands down to the bulge in my lap and quickly unbuttoned my flies as I wrenched off my belt. She drew out my swollen chopper and held it tightly in her hand as it stood up stiffly, twitching slightly as she worked her hand slowly up and down the throbbing shaft.

Our mouths were still glued together as I slipped my hand under her skirt but immediately she pulled my arm down and muttered throatily: 'You naughty boy, Rupert! I haven't quite finished my monthly so we can't consummate our friendship this morning. But I do fancy sucking your delicious-looking cock.'

We rolled about on the rug as I helped Gillian pull down my trousers and drawers and then she sat on my legs, her hands clasping my stiffstander as she bent her head down to kiss the rubicund bare knob. I closed my eyes and groaned with delight as she washed her tongue all around my helmet, nibbling at it with her teeth before gently easing my pulsating prick into her mouth, sucking furiously as instinctively I put up my hands to cup her breasts which swung invitingly before me. Then she placed a hand on my ballsack which sent wave upon wave of exquisite pleasure crashing through my body. I thrust my cock forward and pressed the crown further inside the warm wetness of her mouth.

She was happy to engulf my shaft, sheathing it between her lips and licking and lapping my prick with gay abandon. No man's penis could resist such a cleverly wicked stimulation and I whispered hoarsely that I would be unable to hold back my spend for much longer. I always let this be known for there are girls, admittedly few in number, who enjoy sucking cocks but do not wish to swallow the spunk. I still find this difficult to understand for it can do them no harm whatsoever, but naturally their wishes must always be respected. But as Gillian said later when I mentioned this to her, she adored the taste of sperm and now she nodded as she squeezed my balls through their hairy wrinkled skin and with an immense shudder I expelled my creamy jism which hurtled into her mouth and which she swallowed with evident enjoyment. She sucked my cock with great skill, coaxing out every last drop of jism from my prick until I had been milked dry and she lifted her head with a sigh, smacking her lips in satisfaction.

'Rupert, your spunk has a gratifying tang. Perhaps we could meet at this time tomorrow when I shall be fully ready for you and you may fuck me for as long as you can keep your cock stiff!'

'I look forward to it,' I declared, smiling my approval as we lay motionless, recovering our senses as the autumn breeze cooled our heated bodies. She gave my prick a final friendly rub before I stood up and put my clothes back on. 'Wild horses would not keep me away from you.'

After supper I went to Frank's room where he, Barry and another friend, Leonard Letchmore [*a nephew of the infamous Sir Jonathan Letchmore, a founding member of the fast South Hampstead set which revolved around Count Gewirtz, Sir Ronnie Dunn and Lord Tagholm. He was one of the most infamous rakes of the 1890s of whom it was said that large blue eyes like his might be found in many a stately nursery – Editor*] were gossiping about the events of the previous night. 'I'm sorry in a way that I didn't take up my invitation to Doctor Blayers' party after all,' said Frank. 'Still, I did fuck Nancy and I'm pleased for Barry that he finally got his end away, as the vulgar colloquialism has it.'

'It was good of you, Frank, and I will never forget your kindness – nor that of Rupert, Beth and Esme,' said Barry with some emotion. 'Oh, Rupert, I almost forgot to tell you, the girls sent round a note insisting that they make dinner for us when we see them again. They have suggested next Tuesday which is fine with me. Is it convenient for you? Good, I'll write back tomorrow morning. God, aren't they two smashing girls. I'm so lucky to have met them.'

'Don't get too carried away,' advised Leonard as he poured out glasses of port for us. 'First love can often be idyllic and you were well served. But there are plenty more fish in the sea to be landed, old chap, and as my uncle Sir Jonathan always says, keep playing the sport until you find the special girl with whom you want to stay with for the rest of your life.'

'What, and never fuck any other girl again?' said Frank ironically.

'Supposedly not, though in my uncle's case that practice has certainly never been put into effect! Mind, he's a rogue of the first order though jolly useful as far as I was concerned. I'll wager that few chaps received such a sixteenth birthday present as I was given by Uncle Jonathan.'

'This sounds interesting – tell us more,' I said, settling down in an armchair.

'Well, my birthday is in July and I had just come down from Eton. Actually, my birthday was on the very day I came home and to be honest I was rather miffed to discover that every single one of my relatives and friends, with the sole exception of Uncle Jonathan, had remembered the day and sent me cards and presents. I was especially mortified as he had been perhaps the closest of my many uncles and aunts. But then later that evening I received a hand-delivered letter marked "Strictly Private" and which was delivered to me in great secrecy by our butler, Conway, when my parents were elsewhere in the house, as Uncle Jonathan had previously instructed him. It read:

Dear Leonard,

I haven't forgotten your birthday although it might have so appeared to you. Now you know my flat in Albemarle Street off Piccadilly? We met there in Spring before we went to the theatre with Aunt Anita and your cousins. Be there sharp at three o'clock tomorrow afternoon and you'll have your present. But whatever you do, don't tell

your parents about this or it will spoil the surprise.
Your affectionate uncle,
Jonathan Letchmore

'What was I to make of this note? Naturally, I obeyed his instruction and told my parents the next day that I fancied a brisk constitutional in Green Park. We live in Belgravia so I hailed a cab to take me to Uncle Jonathan's *pied à terre*, which he kept partly as a spare apartment for visitors from abroad as Aunt Anita hails from the United States and partly (as I thought in my naivety) for certain business purposes. As we circumnavigated the hazards of Hyde Park Corner, I racked my brains wondering as to what birthday present Uncle Jonathan had in mind and why it could not be delivered like all the others.

'Despite the usual heavy traffic I arrived there just before the appointed hour and the porter recognised me as he swung open the front door. "Good afternoon, sir, your uncle told me to expect you. He'll be with you later but you're to go right on up and wait for him, if you don't mind." So I took the lift up to the fourth floor and saw to my surprise that the door of Uncle Jonathan's apartment was slightly ajar. This is becoming curiouser by the minute, I said to myself as I pushed it open. There seemed to be no-one else there and one look sufficed to tell me that there had been no burglary. I stood by the sideboard in the lounge and was about to pour myself a sherry when the door from the bedroom opened. Had the flat been visited by robbers after all? I gripped the decanter in my hand, ready to wield it as a weapon.'

He paused dramatically and Frank asked excitedly. 'Go on, Len, who on earth was it? A sneak thief who had managed to climb in from the fire escape?'

'A jolly good guess, Frank, but no, nothing like that – the unexpected visitor had been invited by Uncle Jonathan and she immediately apologised for startling me.'

'It was a woman, then – a friend of your uncle no doubt, who the porter had let in before you,' suggested Barry Jacobs.

Leonard beamed and continued: 'You're getting closer to the mark now. Yes, the porter had let her up to the flat on my uncle's specific instruction. She told me that her name was Fiona but I hardly heard her sweet voice as I gazed upon the pert mass of dark curly hair which had popped round the door. Then a tiny hand brushed the hair away and I could see the most exquisitely beautiful girl framed in the doorway, as pretty as a picture with a face that was somehow disembodied as she smiled, showing pearly white teeth which sparkled in the sunlight that poured through the windows. She came in and shut the door behind her and when I saw her figure, dressed in a loose cotton white dress that was as good as transparent in the bright rays of the sun, I noticed that she was barefoot – and in the back of my mind I somehow thought that I had somewhere before seen this heavenly apparition. ''Hello Leonard, we've never been introduced but I know who you are – and we're not total strangers as you saw me when your uncle took you to the theatre last April," she said, taking my hand in hers. "Ah, were you about to pour yourself a sherry? I think I'll join you if I may."

'Of course! This sweet girl was on the stage of the Alhambra and to her delight I remembered her name and the song she sang so delightfully in the musical show *Berkeley Close*. "You're Fiona Forster and you sang *Love In The Park*," I said with a great effort of memory and she clapped her hands in glee. "Oh Leonard, how clever of you to remember the song. Did you enjoy the show? It's just finished its run after almost ten months at the Alhambra."

' "Very much so, and I remember how well you sang and how pretty you looked on stage," I said, blushing to the roots of my hair. She squealed happily at this compliment. "Oh I can see for sure that you are your uncle's nephew. What a nice compliment and I'm so pleased you could come round to the flat this afternoon.

' "I know why you're here as well. You've come to collect your birthday present," she added roguishly. I looked at her in astonishment and in all innocence asked: "How on earth did you know that?"

' "Goodness me, you silly boy, don't you know? *I'm* your birthday present!" she said happily and in one quick movement she raised her dress over her head and for the very first time in my life I looked in awe at the sensuous beauty of the naked body of a pretty girl. I could hardly believe my eyes as she smoothed her hands over the creamy spheres of her firm breasts. I was rooted to the spot as she pirouetted gaily about the furniture, flaunting her tight rounded bum cheeks and the curly mass of hair which sprouted in a thick triangle at the base of her flat, white belly.

'Then she stood still in front of me and held out her hand. "Come on, Leonard, don't be shy. Come into the bedroom and take off your clothes." I still could not believe what was happening – as if in a dream I followed Fiona into the bedroom and she sat me down on a chair and bent down to unlace my shoes. My heart was pounding, I could feel the perspiration on my forehead but I slowly regained control though surprisingly, even though this delicious nude beauty was peeling off my socks, my prick remained obstinately limp and the thought crossed through my mind that I wouldn't be able to get it up, even though this problem had never occurred during our circle jerks at school or when I had read the copy of *The Temptations Of Cremorne* in the Geography master's study!

' "Didn't naughty Uncle Jonathan even give you a hint of what your present was going to be?" she cooed as she helped me unbutton my shirt. I shook my head and she giggled as she loosened my trousers. In a trice I was naked save for my undershorts. She made me stand up and on her knees slowly pulled down my pants. Perhaps not surprisingly I now felt curiously vulnerable for I was so overcome by a mixture of lust for this gorgeous girl and concern that she might laugh at my fumbling efforts to fuck her that my prick dangled uselessly between my legs.

'But Fiona was wise beyond her years and she whispered: "Don't be nervous, Leonard, it's always a little difficult beginning the race but you'll run well enough once you reach the starting line.'' Slowly at first, she gently stroked my cock and peeled back the foreskin to expose the domed mushroom of my bell-end. This instantly produced the desired effect and as my truncheon stiffened she allowed her fingers to trace a path around and underneath my balls which made my whole body tingle with gratification. After a while she closed her fist around the burgeoning shaft, sliding her fingers along its length until my prick stood up proudly at full erection. ''There, that's a lovely thick tool for such a young boy. It looks good enough to eat,'' she said admiringly and I trembled with joy as, still on her knees, she opened her lips and her pink tongue shot out to lick my shaft from base to tip. I clung to her tousled head as she now kissed my rampant chopper, letting the tip of her tongue flick out to tease my bare knob. Then she opened her mouth wide and encircled my cock with her lips before jamming the throbbing tool inside its heavenly wetness. Her head bobbed down and like a serpent her tongue slid round and round my rod, rolling it cunningly across the swollen knob, and I could feel the playful bite of her pearly teeth as she nipped the sensitive skin of the underside.

'My prick swelled to bursting point and very quickly I spurted a creamy emission into her luscious mouth. She eagerly swallowed every drop of spunk and perhaps because I had spent so quickly my prick was still ramrod stiff as I slowly withdrew it from her lips. The dear girl planted a series of butterfly kisses on my glistening helmet and heaved herself to her feet. "Now for your next lesson," she murmured as she gripped my prick in her hand and led me to the bed. She threw herself down upon it and drew me upon her. I looked down at her exquisite nude body, her slender long legs, her uptilted pointed breasts with the flat belly below which her curly haired pussey glinted in the warm sunshine. I may have lacked any previous experience but Nature told me to take her in my arms and with my mouth on hers I lovingly caressed Fiona's smooth thighs and then raised my hands to rub my fingers against her raised raspberry nipples. But my kind mistress was not yet finished teaching me the refinements of *l'arte de faire l'amour*. "Eat my pussey, Leonard, don't be shy. I adore having my cunney licked out," she panted, pushing my shoulders down with her hands. Again, I had read about this practice in *The Oyster [a spectacularly rude underground magazine — Editor]* but had never had the chance even to attempt it before. In fact, the nearest I had ever come along this path was to French kiss Joanna the parlourmaid and squeeze her breasts through her clothes whilst she rubbed my cock against my flannels.

'Yet by now I had lost much of my nervousness and I prised her legs apart and buried my face between her unresisting thighs. I sniffed her delicate feminine aroma and let my tongue lap freely around the moist curly hair around her cunney lips. She pressed my head forward with her hands and lifted her bottom off the bed, forcing my nose against her cunney. I moved my head slightly upwards and as my hands slipped under her quivering body to clasp her bum cheeks, I slipped my tongue through the pink love lips and licked between the inner grooves of her cunt which was now starting to gush love juice. I tasted her fragrant sweetness, rousing her to new peaks of delight, and I sucked deeply on the pouting cleft that rubbed up and down on my mouth as I tongued her erect, rubbery clitty. Her hands now ran wildly through my hair, pressing on my temples as if to direct this onslaught. She exploded as I continued licking and lapping, swallowing her salty fluids as her hips and bottom moved in synchronised rhythm with my mouth. My face rubbed against her curly bush as she screamed again with delight and, heaving violently, Fiona managed to achieve a second spend before pushing my face away from her juicy crack.

' "Fuck me, Leonard! Oh, you must fuck me now!" she gasped as she drew me up until my face was level with hers. Then, throwing her arms around my neck, she drew my lips to hers as she thrust her wicked tongue into my mouth with all the wild abandon of love, shoving her backside upwards to meet my charge. But I was so excited at the thought that I was about to fuck my first girl that I could not find the entrance to her cunney! I jabbed my hips backwards and forwards, moaning with frustration as I failed to sink my shaft into the eagerly moistened channel that awaited it. Fiona opened her legs wider to make it easier for me. She placed her hand around my raging cock and directed it towards the waiting gap. I sighed as I felt the first thrilling sensation as it eased between the puffy outer lips of her cunt. This was all the help I required and like an iron bolt my prick battered through the cunney flesh, separating the folds of sticky skin and fucking deeper and deeper as my throbbing tool plunged into her, stretching the resilient love channel to its utmost. She spread her legs and bent her knees so that her heels rested upon the small of my back. I pressed home slowly and I marvelled at the wonderful sensations produced on my swollen staff by her tight little cunney. I began to find a rhythm and fucked her with long, simple strokes, glorying in the electric tingle that spread up and down my spine as I slowly withdrew my glistening pole before plunging it right back in.

'If I may say so without seeming smug, we both enjoyed my first fuck, for Fiona was an excellent teacher, slowing me down and then urging me to quicken the pace as her juices lubricated her cunney walls, making my shaft squelch merrily in and out of her honeypot. She twined her legs about my waist and asked me to put my hands under her hips as I pushed forward and buried the entire length of my cock in her hungry snatch. As I did so she began to rub her clitty hard against my rigid rod and her soft moans turned to a rising scream as she urged me on. "A-h-r-e! You dear boy, push on! Come now, Leonard, empty your balls!" she cried out and I began to pump wildly, feeling my ballsack smack against her bottom as together we scaled the heights of ecstacy. I crashed huge shoots of love cream into her sopping cunney and this brought down her flow of pussey juice, which flooded her luscious nest, and our fluids oozed down in a trickle across her thighs.

'We lay panting as I slowly withdrew my glistening cock which was still almost as stiff as before it first entered her glorious quim. When we had recovered our senses she began to fondle my cock and her hand moved rhythmically up and down my stiffening shaft between her long fingers. As my prick hardened I felt myself being pushed upon my back and Fiona said: "There are other ways to enjoy fucking, Leonard. I particularly like being on top because it allows my clitty to be rubbed by the tip of the cock but some men, rather foolishly to my way of thinking, find it demeaning in some way to be beneath a female during love-making. Mind, these are the rough kind of fellows I would never let get in between my legs. Still, that's another story. Let me show you what I mean about the girl-on-top position."

'She climbed up on top of me, bending forward to kiss my lips as I cupped those voluptuous breasts in my hands, feeling the hard little titties against my palms. Her oily cunney lips were just touching the very tip of my helmet, which made my staff tremble with anticipation. When she moved her hips so that her cunney lips slid over my knob, I thrilled in the clinging wetness as she lowered herself gently until almost all of my throbbing length was inside her. "There, isn't that nice?" she asked, and I gasped back how perfectly splendid it was as she raised herself up and then suddenly plumped herself down hard, impaling herself on my cock which revelled in its surround of warm, wet cunney flesh.

'How she squealed as she moved her body up and down, using her thighs to ride me, bobbing herself up and down so that her breasts jounced up and down as I met her downward thrusts with jerks of my hips upwards. I panted heavily with this exertion as Fiona heaved herself up and down on my twitching tool, taking every last inch of me deep into her hairy pit, and the continuous nipping and contractions of her clever pussey soon brought me to a rip-roaring spend. At first I tried to hold back but I could not deny the boiling spunk that was racing up from my balls and I sent a tremendous jet of jism up into her cunt as she rocked up and down, faster and faster until with a delighted yell she writhed in convulsions of joy as her orgasm enveloped her body and she shivered all over, almost swooning away as her cunney disgorged a rivulet of love fluids all over my matted pubic thatch.

' "Well, what do you think, Lenny, was that as good as before?" she gasped as she rolled off me to lay panting in my arms. "Just as good if not even better," I replied truthfully. "I read somewhere that this method is known as the lazy man's fuck and I can see why. You have to do most of the work."

'But before she could answer we were startled by a fruity chuckle from our right. "Well now, you look as if you've been working well enough already, nephew," commented the gentleman whose portly frame filled the doorway. It was none other than Uncle Jonathan himself! "I'm glad to see that my birthday present has been

72

opened," he continued, smacking his lips with evident gusto.

' "He's a chip off the old block and fully deserved his treat," said Fiona. "Oh, do come in, Jonathan, if you are staying and shut the door. I want to fuck Leonard again so you'll have to share if you want to join us."

' "I will with pleasure," said my randy uncle who tore off his clothes with an amazing rapidity and in a trice was on the bed with us, his veiny cock heavy as it lay semi-erect over his thigh. "After all, there's nothing like keeping it in the family." I motioned as if to leave but Fiona caught my arm. "No, no, don't go – let's see if I can stiffen you up to ride your cock again, and while we're at it your uncle can fuck my bum if he can't get in my cunt," she suggested.

' "Sounds like a good idea," agreed Uncle Jonathan, reaching out for a pot of cold cream whilst Fiona knelt down and popped my cock into her mouth. Could I rise to the occasion one more time? Her darting tongue moved along my rod and as she licked my knob my shaft began to grow and swell up as hard and as stiff as ever. She gave my cock one last long lick and said: "Oooh, what stamina – I envy the lucky girl who'll be fucked by you now you've got the hang of it."

'In no time at all she was back between my legs, her cunney lips slipping over my knob in an instant, and she bounced up and down, repeating the pleasure as Uncle Jonathan tried to insert his thick member in her cunt alongside mine, but this was impossible to achieve. So my uncle clamped his hands on her arse and parted her rounded bum cheeks and then he dipped a hand into the cold cream and liberally anointed her rear dimple. Fiona stuck out her bottom as he wet his sizeable knob with yet another dollop of cold cream. Then he pushed his thick shaft between her buttocks and soon his vigorous shoves gained an entrance as Fiona wiggled her bum lasciviously in front of him, enjoying the feel of his domed knob which was well burrowed inside her backside. Clamping her firmly, Uncle Jonathan pushed forward until his entire shaft was sheathed inside her back passage. For a brief moment we rested with our two cocks throbbing against the other with only the thin divisional membrane of the anal canal separating them.

'Then I started to jerk my body up and down, my cock sluicing through her engorged quim whilst Fiona wriggled her *derrière* in time with each sliding motion of Uncle Jonathan's lusty organ. I found this threesome fucking so exciting that I came very soon after, injecting soul-stirring spurts of spunk, and this led to Uncle Jonathan pumping his prick in and out of Fiona's bum at a fast rate of knots until he ejaculated a hot gush of juice into her bottom. He gallantly withdrew his prick slowly until with an audible plop! the avuncular tool emerged and he sank back, mopping his brow. "Phew, that was fun," he grunted. "Now who would like a drink?"

'I spent the rest of the afternoon and evening with Jonathan and Fiona, my kindly uncle telephoning my parents to say that he was taking me out to supper as a birthday treat, which was in fact the case, although I dare say Uncle Jonathan could be justly accused of being economical with the truth!'

Frank slowly expelled a great breath of air. 'Damn it, I wish I had an uncle like yours, you lucky blighter.'

'Yes, he's a real good sport, and on my seventeenth birthday he took me to a Victor Pudendum contest at the Jim Jam Club *[a notorious meeting place in Great Windmill Street where the very highest in the land took part in discreet affairs and wild orgies – Editor]*. I must be going now as I have to prepare some notes for a tutorial,' said Leonard, rising to his feet, 'but all of you please remember, if any of you ever find yourselves short of a good fuck in London, just call me. I'm now an associate member of the Jim Jam and for just ten bob *[fifty pence – Editor]* Solly the doorman can always be relied on to provide a couple of pretty young dollymops.'

'I'd better leave too as I also have work to prepare for tomorrow,' I said, though thinking more of my assignments with Beth, Esme and Gillian than the boring pages of my books on political economy. 'See you at breakfast, chaps,' I added as I strolled back to my room with a smile on my face, as it suddenly struck me how funny it would be for one of my uncles, the Rector of West Finchley, to be offered an evening at the Jim Jam Club. However, the old boy was no fool and whilst passing the port after dinner one evening whilst a guest at our house, he made it clear that before marriage he had himself enjoyed what he described as 'The Fleshpots Of The Metropolis', and that he considered it right and proper for any young man to enjoy some happy years of freedom. 'Mind, I cannot countenance over-familiar dalliances with young, attractive members of the opposite, ah, gender.' I listened in respectful silence, stifling my amusement when he proceeded to lean over and in a conspiratorial whisper murmured in my ear: 'But if you do find yourself tempted by the sins of the flesh, my advice is to go for a girl with large titties. For as we often said in officers' mess when I served with the Hussars: like titties, like clitty.'

Of course, by that time Uncle Arthur had downed the best part of a full decanter of '96 Old and Crusted so to be fair, it was the port rather than the clergyman giving me that sound advice!

I shook myself free of this pleasant reverie as I opened the door to my quarters. For a moment I thought I had entered the wrong room for Nancy the maid was lying on my bed, dressed only in a flimsy nightdress and lying on her tummy. Alongside her, completely naked, was a most attractive tall girl, finely formed with blonde hair falling down in ringlets onto her shoulders. She had smaller breasts than the generously endowed Nancy but possessed firm, chubby buttocks which quivered as she lifted her head and said: 'Nancy, is this the young gentleman you were talking about before supper?'

'Yes, this is Rupert Mountjoy,' said Nancy, waving her hand lazily at me. 'Rupert, I want you to meet my friend Rosa Crouthampe, who works at Brasenose College but comes over to visit me as often as she can. Rosa is my very best friend, aren't you, dearest? Isn't she pretty,

Rupert? Look at the rolling swell of her bum cheeks. Now turn over, Rosa, and let Rupert see the tight yellow curls around your cunney and the dear little love lips peeking through them. Wouldn't you like to plonk your big cock between them, Rupert, you randy devil? Oh dear, you must forgive my naughty language but we've had a few drinks to celebrate my birthday, and anyhow, I'm sure you'd want to fuck Rosa because you and Barry and Frank are the randiest boys out of all the first year students.'

'You're very probably right,' I agreed as I shut the door behind me.

'But you shouldn't speak to Rupert in such a familiar way and I think you owe him an apology,' said Rosa, and despite my protestations that I was not in the least offended by Nancy's remark, Rosa insisted that Nancy should be punished for her indiscreet observations. Nancy herself did not seem to want to challenge her friend on this point and offered no resistance when Rosa turned her over on her belly and, throwing up her chemise, exposed Nancy's perfectly rounded little bum cheeks to my lascivious gaze. She then rose to her knees and began to smack the two beautiful white hemispheres of Nancy's backside, saying: 'This will teach you to be so forward, you bad girl.' She slapped lightly and it was plain that both girls were enjoying this little scene. Rosa's lithe naked body glistened as her hand rose and fell, her round, nut-brown nipples rising and falling quickly with each sharp stroke, her cheeks slightly flushed with her exertions and her blue eyes sparkling with excitement as she chastised her naughty friend.

'Oh! Oh! Oh! No more, Rosa, ouch, it hurts, it hurts, Ouch! Please stop!' begged Nancy as she winced and wriggled under the rapid succession of slaps.

'Quiet now, Nancy! Stop making such a fuss,' snapped Rosa fiercely. 'You have been a very bad girl and all bad girls get smacked. Besides, Rupert and I love the way your bum cheeks jiggle as I smack them. Now we want to see your lovely botty colour up. See how nicely your buttocks are blushing! They should always be bright pink, shouldn't they, Rupert?'

This lewd scene had made my cock swell up unbearably and as I watched this stimulating scene Nancy called out to me: 'Come on then, show us your stiffstander.' The thought flashed through my mind of what would occur if we were caught (for there were no locks on the doors) but as the maxim of the great Count Gewirtz of Galicia has it: *ven der putz shtayt, ligt seichel oif'n fenster [when the prick stands up, common sense flies out the window – Editor]* and I shucked off my clothes in record time. I jumped onto the bed and huddled up next to Rosa who, without missing one beat of her rhythm as she continued her inexorable spanking of Nancy's now tingling backside, clamped her wide, red lips around my rampant cock.

Mercifully for the other girl, this excited Rosa so much that after bobbing her head back and forth to suck in as much of my shaft as she could, she ceased her slapping of Nancy's poor bum and instead she jammed her hands around my pulsating prick which already had a blob of milky jism formed on the tip of my knob. She jammed down the foreskin and lashed her tongue round my pole which was now thudding away like a steamhammer. I worked my hips backwards and forwards as her pliant tongue washed over my bared helmet, thoroughly enjoying this delicious sucking-off.

Meanwhile Nancy had raised herself on her hands and knees and had lowered her pretty head between Rosa's legs, splaying open her buttocks to make room for her lips to kiss between the ripe, white globes, worrying her tongue around her corn-coloured pussey hair which I imagined was already dampening with love juice, teasing the tip around the pouting pussey lips before slipping in and out of her juicy quim.

Fired by this tribadic activity I pulled my prick away from Rosa's mouth and positioned myself behind Nancy, whose rounded bottom cheeks were moving in rhythm as she suctioned Rosa's blonde-haired pussey between her lips. Nancy took hold of my sinewy shaft with her right hand and directed its purple-domed head to the glorious vale between her buttocks and to the tight-looking wrinkled hole that lay between them. After further wetting my tool with spittle, I attacked this fortress with vigour, but as my member forced its way past the sphincter muscle she wailed: 'Ah, stop! Stop! You'll rend me if you don't withdraw!' Fortunately I keep a small jar of pomade [*a perfumed ointment for the hair – Editor*] on the bedside table so I swiftly greased my cock and again set my knob at the little brown bum-hole. The pomade worked like a charm for this time when I pushed forward Nancy wriggled her arse until I was firmly ensconced inside her bum.

For a brief moment I rested and then slowly began to pull in and out whilst I threw my arms around her waist and frigged her pussey. Nancy responded to this double stimulation by squirming under the surging strokes of my prick. Her legs began to shake and I knew that her spend was approaching. She gripped hold of Rosa's thighs as she lapped furiously at the girl's soaking slit. Nancy's juices flowed freely and she worked her bum to bring me off, and I flooded her arse with a copious discharge of sperm which both warmed and lubricated her superb bottom. As I spunked into her I continued to work my prick back and forth so that it remained as hard as rock as, with a 'pop', I uncorked my tool from her bum-hole. We screamed loudly in the frenzy of emission as Rosa also spent over Nancy's lapping tongue and we collapsed in a heap on my bed.

When we had recovered Nancy thanked me for taking the trouble to use the pomade and not simply pushing forward and ignoring her plea to withdraw. 'I sometimes think that there are some men who enjoy hurting their partners – or at best they are uncaring,' she complained. 'Most girls enjoy a good fuck up the bum but only when the cock has been well oiled beforehand with butter or some other substance.' Since this day I have heeded her words and have always kept a jar of cold cream handy for this purpose. But now we were fired up again and we engaged in some splendid three way kisses, pressing our lips together and waggling our tongues around in a most sensuous manner. If we had had any inhibitions they were now cast aside, so I had not the slightest intention of ducking the challenge when Nancy placed her hand on top of my head and drew it down towards Rosa's hairy mound, saying: 'Rosa loves having her pussey kissed. I've brought her off, Rupert, now let's see if you can do so.'

I drew my body up until my tongue was level with her titties and began by nibbling at her nipples, licking and sucking on their rubbery hardness until they were sticking out like two tiny stalks. Then I let my tongue travel slowly down the velvety white skin of her tummy, pausing briefly to encircle her belly-button before sliding down into the curly smooth hair of her mound. Like a snake I slid myself down between her legs as I parted her soft, lightly scented pubic bush with my fingertips to reveal her swollen clitoris, and as I worked my lips into the long gash of her cleft I breathed in the delicious aroma from her clean, appealing cunney, a fragrance which has always greatly excited me. By slipping a hand under her bum, I pressed her even more closely to me as I placed my lips directly over her clitty and sucked it into my mouth, where the tip of my tongue began to explore it from all directions. I could feel it growing even larger as her heels drummed against the sheets and her legs twitched up and down along the sides of my body.

Rosa became hugely agitated when I found the tiny button under the fold at the base of her clitty and began twirling my tongue around it. The faster I vibrated my tongue, the more she twisted and turned and I was forced to move both of my hands to her shoulders to keep her cunney pressed against my face. She now started to gyrate her pelvis as I increased the stimulation and she planted her feet firmly on my back as if she desired to mould our two bodies into one mass of quivering flesh.

'Oooh! Aaah! Stick your cock in me now!' panted Rosa, and this was an opportunity my bursting prick was happy to take. So I heaved myself up and fixed my lips on one of her horned-up nipples, and the strawberry stalk grew long and hard as I sucked it between my teeth. At the same time her cunney responded to the urgings of the three fingers I had buried inside the clinging sheath and I frigged her slippery clitty with my thumb. The more I frigged her, the quicker she jerked her hips and she grabbed my cock and began pumping my shaft, sliding her hand up and down in such insane excitement that she spent then and there and I felt the sticky moistness of her honey cascade over my hand. This set me off and I spunked a profuse libation of hot, creamy jism that drenched her hand. She directed my spurting shaft up to her belly and smeared my cream all over her white tummy.

'Now who's been a naughty girl,' stormed Nancy. 'See how you've wasted poor Rupert's semen. Get up and bend over the chair in the corner.' To my surprise, Rosa meekly did as she was told and when she had placed herself over the chair, Nancy gave me one of my slippers and told me to chastise the wayward girl.

'No, I can't do that, Rosa would not want to be spanked,' I laughed nervously as I took a long look at the plump, well-shaped cheeks of Rosa's behind.

'Oh, but Nancy's right,' Rosa called out, turning her head to look at me. 'I have been a bad girl and deserve to have my bum smacked.'

Well, there is no accounting for tastes, and although in my time I have spanked a good number of female bottoms I have never been a fervent devotee of *le vice anglais*. Perhaps this is because at St Lionel's Academy, corporal punishment was unknown and we suffered none of the sadistic beatings inflicted upon pupils at most other English public schools. But be that as it may, whilst I draw the line at really whipping one's partner's backside, if the girl really likes to be stimulated in such fashion, so be it, and I cannot deny that I achieve some mild satisfaction from distributing the occasional few passionate slaps on the swells of feminine rears.

So I jumped out of bed and went across to where Rosa lay inert over the chair, provocatively wiggling her arse as I approached. I passed my hand caressingly over the cool, soft skin of the swelling cheeks of her buttocks. I brought the sole of my slipper down upon these pretty posteriors but my first few strokes hardly changed the colour of the flesh and Rosa turned her head round and said: 'You may hit harder than that, Rupert. Honestly, I can hardly feel anything.'

'Are you certain that this is what you want?' I asked, 'Because if it is, my girl, I'll give it to you!' She nodded and so this time I lifted my arm high and brought down the slipper with a thwack which must have made her bottom tingle. I struck her again in similar smart fashion and her bum cheeks soon assumed a glowing, rosy hue as I administered a good, sound spanking. This pleased both girls for Nancy went down on her knees and sucked up my cock between her lips, palating my prick so sensuously that my shaft swelled up to bursting point in her mouth. After a dozen strokes I threw away the slipper and led Rosa back to the bed where, as I surmised she would find her backside too painful to lie upon, I pushed her face downwards, her legs apart but on the floor and her forearms on the bed. She knew what was about to happen so she stuck out her backside for me to part the two tingling cheeks and I plunged my trusty cock into her warm, juicy slit from behind, my balls fairly cracking against her bottom.

'Keep going, that's the ticket!' she laughed merrily, and her backside responded to every shove as I pounded her pussey, driving home until, excited to such raging peaks, the contractions of her deliciously tight cunney lips sucked the spunk from my prick. The sweet friction of her pussey lips against the sensitive skin of my knob sent the sperm pumping through my shaft into her waiting love box as I thrust my twitching tool to and fro with all my youthful vigour.

Nancy threw herself down to lie beside us on her back, her hands busy parting her pussey lips as she frigged herself excitedly, somehow managing to turn her head across to lick Rosa's goregous titties. My own climax was nearing and our surging cries of joy echoed around the room as the three of us began the journey down the road to ecstacy. Then I started to tremble and began shaking like a leaf from head to toe, until a huge wave of delight flooded through my body and I sent thick wads of creamy spunk crashing into Rosa's sopping cunney and she too screamed with delight as she shivered through a powerful orgasm just as the hot, frothy jism drenched her womb.

Well, of course I would have liked nothing better than to have continued to fuck both girls throughout the remainder of the evening. But I had an important essay to prepare for Professor Webb and reluctantly ordered the girls to leave my room and go back downstairs. They were most disappointed and even my insistence on giving each of the girls a pound note as a farewell present did not mollify them.

'I bet you've already found some posh tart from one of the women's colleges. These girls are supposed to arrive here all sweet and innocent but it doesn't take them long to snap up any young boy who has had some experience and knows how to fuck like a gentleman,' sighed Nancy. 'Rupert, don't forget now, any time you want your cock sucked, please let me know.'

I smiled my goodbyes and with difficulty turned my mind to such stimulating legal matters as the rights of landlords and tenants and the ramifications of the judgement in the case of The Attorney General versus The Borough of Fulham in the High Court fifteen years ago. It was devilishly hard to concentrate upon such affairs. When I banished Nancy and Rosa from my mind, Beth and Esme stepped up smartly to take their place and when I finally forced them out of my brain, a picture of the beautiful Gillian Headleigh formed itself every time I tried to focus my eyes on the page. My heart began to pound as I remembered her words: *'meet me at this time tomorrow and you may fuck me for as long as you can keep your cock stiff!'* The old, familiar tingling began to make itself felt in my groin. My hand wandered down to smooth itself over my shaft, but I had no need of the five-fingered widow after tonight's fun and games, and anyhow I needed to keep up my strength for Gillian tomorrow morning. So I cleared my mind of everything except the need to prepare for Professor Webb's tutorial and doggedly read six more pages from my textbook, scribbling some notes and memorising some important points before slamming the book shut, and after a refreshing warm bath I settled down in bed, as happy as a sandboy.

As is still my custom, I picked up a newspaper to read for a few minutes before turning off the light and in the *Oxford Mail* my attention was captured by a report of the speech made at the Empire Club by Dr Whibley of Merton College attacking 'the monstrous encroachment of women upon the University' and how a mixed University – 'the dream of the farcemonger' – will lose its unique distinction. 'The University will be destroyed because once more the patent truth has been ignored that men are men and women women.'

For how long will such reactionary views be propounded in this new twentieth century, I thought to myself as I chucked the newspaper on the floor in disgust, because no force on earth can turn back the clock once a sizeable proportion of the population (for better or worse) refuse to accept the old established order. By and large, women will never again be content with a subservient role in society despite the rantings of Dr Whibley and his ilk, and will rightly demand the same privileges and duties as men.

As far as I was concerned, it was a most pleasant discovery to find out that inside the ivy-covered college walls, away from the prying gaze of the outside world, the opportunity arose for many girls to shed a cloak of modesty which could be safely stripped away. My first days in Oxford, alone and apprehensive as to whether I would be happy spending three years here, were miserable indeed – but after meeting these jolly girls who revelled in their new-found freedom, there was now no doubt in my mind that the student life had much to commend itself to a red-blooded young man who enjoyed the taste of forbidden fruit!

CHAPTER TWO

Extramural Studies

MY HEART SANK WHEN DURING BREAKFAST the following morning a college servant presented me with a letter which had been hand-delivered by a young lady just half an hour beforehand. 'Damn and blast!' I muttered as I gave myself the mental odds of a pound to a penny that the envelope contained a note from Gillian cancelling our mid-day tryst.

At first glance my pessimism seemed to have been well-founded for indeed the letter was from this pretty girl and as I had forecast, she could not meet me as planned. But as I read on my face broke into a smile for this was no mere cold cancellation but a hot-blooded *billet-doux* which I still have in my possession and so can reproduce it in full:

Dearest Rupert,
First, the bad news; I cannot meet you as planned this morning because I have to attend a lecture which has been brought forward from four o'clock this afternoon.

But this leaves me free from one o'clock and at the risk of sounding over-forward I would like to suggest that we meet for a late luncheon at Carlo's Restaurant which is in Woodstock Road just before the junction with Little Clarendon Street. If the weather is good we could take a bus or train to Woodstock and see Blenheim Palace [A richly furnished palace with many art treasures designed by Sir John Vanbrugh for the Duke of Marlborough and mostly paid for by Parliament in recognition of the Duke's victory over the French at the Battle of Blenheim in the War of the Spanish Succession – Editor].

On the other hand, if it's raining, we could go back to my house as, like yesterday, my room-mates will be away until at least six o'clock. Somehow, even if the sun is shining brightly, I think I can speculate what you would prefer to do and oh, Rupert, to be honest, I wouldn't be too disappointed if we went to Blenheim Palace on another day!

For if I were forced to make a choice between viewing the marvellous Blenheim gardens laid out by Capability Brown [a noted eighteenth-century landscape gardener – Editor] *and sucking your cock, I would always plump for the latter. I do love sucking a fat juicy prick, caressing the red mushroomed crown with my lips and then washing it with my tongue. It is so thrilling when the shaft trembles in my mouth and so exciting when the frothy cream shoots out of the tiny hole and I can spread the sticky jism all around the knob with my tongue. I love swallowing mouthfuls of tangy spunk too and cannot think of anything that tastes so fine and clean.*

Enough now, for writing this frank confession is making my pussey damp and soon it will be crying out for relief which I can only partially satisfy by frigging myself. Only a proud, throbbing stiffstander like yours will be able to quench my voracious sensual desires . . .

If you aren't free this afternoon, leave a note at my house. Otherwise, I'll be at Carlo's restaurant at around twenty past one this afternoon and look forward to seeing you there.
Love,
Gillian

Well, dear reader, I doubt whether you would have to ponder for more than a second about a choice between walking round Blenheim Palace or fucking Gillian Headleigh! The only problem facing me now was how to collect my thoughts for Professor Simon Webb's tutorial which would begin in ten minutes' time. Somehow I managed to concentrate upon my work and after what seemed an eternity the hands of the clock finally came together at noon. I gathered my books up in a rush and was about to fly out the room when the Professor beckoned me. 'Mr Mountjoy, a quick word if you have a moment,' he said and though I could hardly wait to get back to my room to change I could hardly refuse to listen to a senior lecturer.

'I am inviting a few undergraduates over for an after dinner soirée in my quarters tomorrow night and I wonder whether you would care to join us at about half past eight?' This was an honour indeed and I accepted his invitation with sincere pleasure, especially as he had not, as I had feared, engaged in further discussion upon our work, which was just as well because already I had little time to spruce myself up before my appointment with the lovely Gillian at Carlo's Restaurant.

In fact I arrived at Carlo's in good time and was welcomed effusively by the eponymous owner, Signor Carlo Justini, who has of course since found fame and fortune as the proprietor of the Trattoria d'Argento in Piccadilly which is patronised by the *crème de la crème* of London Society. 'Come this way, sir. Miss 'Eadleigh has booked a table in a private room upstairs. Perhaps you would like a glass of wine whilst you wait for her?' he suggested, but before I could even answer him Gillian had entered the restaurant and I greeted her. In front of Carlo we exchanged a formal handshake, though once he had brought us a bottle of chilled white wine and taken our order, I leaned over the table and kissed her firmly on the lips.

'Thank you for your lovely letter,' I said as I resumed my seat, 'but you win no prizes for guessing what I prefer to do after luncheon.'

'You mean then that I shall have to wait for another occasion to walk round Blenheim Palace,' she said, returning my smile. 'Well, I think I can live with this disappointment so long as you can provide me with an equally pleasurable entertainment this afternoon.'

'Gillian, I promise you that will prove to be no problem,' I assured her as our eyes met in a knowing glance and, when I felt her foot rub sinuously against my ankle, I knew that this sensuous girl was feeling just as randy as me! But there was no huge hurry for we had until six o'clock to ourselves and we first enjoyed a delicious luncheon, the highlight of which was grilled chicken with a *panzanella* bread salad of plum tomatoes and parsley. We both ate sparingly for we knew that fucking on a full stomach is not a practice to be recommended. As we sipped our *grappa*, the little minx must have slipped off her shoes for I felt her silk-clad foot move up between my legs under the cover of the sparkling white linen tablecloth. Gillian giggled as Signor Justini bustled in with a fresh pot of coffee and she stroked the stiff length of my shaft with her toes.

'Have you ever fucked in a restaurant, Rupert?' she whispered throatily as her toes continued to stroke my stiffstander.

'No, but I'm more than willing to try out the experience,' I replied.

Gillian leaned forward and as she was wearing a jacket with a low neckline, I was given a clear view of her firm, ripe breasts. 'Well, it's very nice to repair to a couch immediately after leaving the table, but as there is a nice, comfortable bed waiting round the corner, perhaps it would be as well to wait until another time. I do have a fondness for such sport you see, because it was in a private dining-room such as this at the Café Clive that I became a woman.

'Yes, Rupert,' she continued. 'I was first fucked by Sir Andrew Stuck, perhaps the randiest rogue in all London.'

'I hope he did not take advantage of you,' I

commented, for even then I knew that an extra bottle of champagne often led to a remorseful morning.

'Oh no, I was more than willing to surrender my virginity to him. I was like the Lady of Kent in the limerick:

There was a young Lady of Kent,
Who said that she knew what it meant
When men asked her to dine
And also to wine,
She knew what it meant — but she went!'

I was keenly interested to hear more but Signor Justini knocked on the door and presented us with the bill. As I busied myself writing out a cheque, Gillian muttered: 'I'll tell you more about it when we get home, although you must fuck me first.'

'Your wish is my command,' I replied quietly as Signor Justini and his staff ushered us out into the street. It was less than five minutes' walk to Gillian's rooms and, as she had promised in her letter, none of the other girls in the house were present. We ran straight up to the bedroom and in an inkling we had shucked off our clothes and embraced each other's naked body as we rolled around on the soft mattress.

'My darling boy! Tell me how you are going to fuck me,' she cried.

I thought for a moment and said: 'How am I going to fuck you, Gillian? Well, first I am going to roll you over on your back and then I shall mount you as I decide which way we shall first take our pleasure. To begin with, perhaps I shall simply lie on your belly and slowly insert my long, thick cock into your inviting little wet snatch. Then I'll push forward until my shaft is fully inside your velvety sheath before I pull it out and then tease the lips of your pussey with my knob. Then I'll crash my cock back inside your cunney and pump away, increasing the tempo gradually until I'm pistoning such hard, deep thrusts that my balls crack against your thighs. Then we'll come together, my throbbing tool spewing out a sea of sperm whilst your pussey creams itself with the sweet love juices from your hairy honeypot.'

'What a magnificent fuck that sounds! But let me first salute your proud prick.' She dived down to brush my iron-hard member with her cheek as she licked my heavy, hanging balls with her wet tongue. I writhed in delicious agony as she transferred her attentions to my cock, licking the shaft from base to tip in long, langorous strokes. She moved round to make herself comfortable as she played with my prick, pressing it to each of her smallish but beautifully rounded breasts, squeezing it between them and then softly biting and tickling my purple knob with the end of her wicked little tongue. Then suddenly she thrust her mouth down and took my entire eight inches into her mouth and her salacious sucking almost brought me off there and then.

It was far too early to shoot my load so I placed my hands gently under her shoulders and heaved her back onto the bed until she was lying down and she whispered: 'Suck on my titties, please, Rupert, this really makes me feel very randy.' She spoke the truth for she started to squirm as soon as my lips touched her stalky nip. As I sucked it into my mouth I ran my hands all over her body, lingering on her inner thighs whilst I took one and then the other rubbery red tittie between my lips, licking and lapping at the succulent flesh as Gillian's hand now circled and slid up and down my raging staff. Then it was her turn to pull my body upwards as she parted her long, slim legs and as I entered her I paused to savour the sensation as my mushroom helmet squelched its way inside her damp, soft-walled tunnel. She raised her legs high as our loins locked together, our hips bucking wildly as we thrashed around and I pounded in and out, my hands clasping the firm white globes of her backside as the spunk boiled up in my balls and thrust upwards through my pulsating penis.

Alas, I simply could not wait for Gillian to climax and with a mighty groan I flooded her cunt with a torrent of warm sperm as jets of jism poured out of my prick so abundantly that her thighs were well lubricated. I withdrew my tingling truncheon, rubbing it amorously against the sticky lips of her pussey.

'Oh dear, I am so sorry,' I apologised as I rolled over to cuddle her in my arms, 'but I just could not hold back any longer.'

'There is absolutely no need to apologise, you sweet boy. You fucked me delightfully and I don't have to spend every time, you know,' she said generously.

'But surely it *does* matter,' I persisted. 'If you don't manage to climax then I must be doing something wrong.'

Gillian sat up and put a finger against my mouth. 'Let me give you some good advice, Rupert. You really must not become obsessed with timing your spend or you will be in danger of forgetting everything else! Although I grant you that some men do have a problem about spending too quickly, I assure you there is very little to be gained in holding back or forcing forward merely to achieve a simultaneous spend.

'Of course it can be great fun to climax together but this is but one joy of love-making which need never interfere with any other pleasures. Why, I've often found that spending at different times allows the partner who comes first to concentrate on exciting the other which can be very, very nice for them both.'

Maybe I still looked doubtful for she added: 'Rupert, if you don't believe me, I'll gladly lend you my copy of that marvellous textbook *Fucking For Beginners* by Nigel Andrews and you'll read for yourself that what I am telling you is plain, simple fact.'

Of course as I matured I soon realised the complete truth of Gillian's words though at the time they were spoken I did believe that she was perhaps slightly gilding the lily for my benefit. Anyway, I nodded my head in agreement and quickly changed the subject. 'What about telling me instead the story of how you were fucked by Sir Andrew Stuck?' I demanded as I threw my arm around her shoulders.

She giggled and said: 'Oh yes, I mentioned something about my first poking by young randy Andy at the restaurant, didn't I? It was quite an adventure really as naturally I was still at Trippett's Academy. I had come home for the Easter holidays and I decided to visit my friend Estelle Kenton, who happens to be Andrew's cousin. I'd never met Andrew although like most girls of our class living in London I had heard of his reputation as a ladies' man. As luck would have it, Andrew had also decided to visit Estelle that fateful afternoon and when I was introduced to him I could see why so many young women (as rumour had it) offered themselves for his delectation. There's no getting away from the fact that he's a handsome chap with a friendly face and a witty turn of speech.

'Andrew is one of those chaps who is so blessed with the gift of the gab that if fate had placed him in a different strata of society he would have made an excellent career as a salesman in one of these new huge emporiums in the West End.

'To cut short a long story, before he left us, Andrew asked me to dine with him the following evening. Normally I would have had to ask permission from my parents but they were spending a few days away in the country with some friends so I was free to accept Andrew's invitation without any hindrance. He called for me punctually at eight o'clock in his new motor vehicle and as Grahame, his chauffeur, drove through Oxford Street Andrew told me that he had booked a table at the Café Clive in Museum Street, Bloomsbury. Now I had read about this establishment in the illustrated papers and knew it to be a favourite haunt of the smart 'fast' set, and this already added an extra spice to the evening.

'When we arrived there was already quite a gathering at the restaurant as Lord George Lucas had booked a table to celebrate his birthday. Along with a clutch of other young men his party consisted of chorus girls from the musical comedy at the Alhambra Theatre which was due to open in three days' time. This merry throng dominated the atmosphere but I found it all terribly exciting, especially when the handsome Lord George himself came up to our table. "Hello, Andrew, you lucky so-and-so. How in heaven's name did you manage to persuade this gorgeous young lady to dine with you tonight?

' "I don't think I've had the pleasure," he added as he turned to me, his sensuous grey eyes locked into mine, and I smiled demurely, trying hard to act the part of a shy, blushing maiden.

' "Yes you have, George, but not with that pretty girl," called out one of his friends from his table. "At least, not yet!"

'Andrew was not overpleased by Lord George's intervention especially when the young peer invited us to join his party, and he murmured his thanks after I had politely declined and Lord George returned to his guests, where his jolly friend Mr Stockman was regaling the company with a risqué story about how he had recently encountered a pretty young woman who turned out to be a witch whilst driving his carriage along a country lane. He knew she was a witch for when she put her hand on the front of his trousers he turned into a lay-by!

'We enjoyed a splendid meal and then Andrew suggested that we took our coffee and liqueurs in one of the small private rooms upstairs. Monsieur Clive himself ushered us into the room which was richly decorated with fine furnishings. I noticed immediately that what appeared to be suspiciously like a bed frame and mattress stood in a corner, covered in cream linen sheets along with two big matching pillows plumped up against the wall. I said nothing but sat across the table from Andrew who poured out two steaming cups of black coffee as he asked me whether I would care to join him in a glass of cognac or some other liqueur from the clutch of bottles on the small sideboard. I accepted his offer of coffee and chose a kummel [a Central European aniseed and cumin liqueur favoured by Queen Victoria – Editor] to accompany it.

'We held hands as we talked and Andrew must have slipped off a shoe for I felt his foot insinuate itself between my ankles and I was so aroused as his toes moved higher and higher that my silk knickers were soon damp even before his foot had reached my thighs!

'I shall spare us both further blushes except to admit that I was no match for Andrew Stuck's polished technique of seduction. In my defence I shall simply say that few girls could resist the charms of this handsome, wealthy young baronet and very shortly afterwards he moved round to sit next to me and we exchanged a passionate kiss. As his tongue probed inside my mouth I felt his hand fondling my breasts. "What divine bosoms, Gillian. I am sure your titties will be as beautiful to the eye as they are to the touch."

'After this sweet compliment Andrew unbuttoned my dress and gently eased off the front of my chemise so that my naked breasts lay in his hands. We kissed again and he squeezed my nipples so wonderfully that they became hard and pointed. He rubbed them between his fingers and as he stroked them he put his head down and began to kiss and suck my erect little red soldiers.

'Soon I was lying naked and trembling on the bed watching him undress and admiring his wiry, athletic body – and no doubt like so many girls before and after this experience, I gasped with wonderment when he pulled down his drawers to reveal his astonishingly thick prick which sprang upwards from the mass of black hair at the base of his belly. Although technically I was still a virgin (though I had often used the ladies' comforter I had purchased by mail-order from Madame Nettleton's – you must have seen their advertisements in *Society News* with their famous guarantee that "all purchases are sent in discreet plain parcels" – and had previously frigged and sucked a certain number of cocks) I knew that Andrew would want to fuck me, but I was worried that I could never accommodate that enormous shaft inside my little cunney.

'Andrew took me in his arms as he knelt down and laid down beside me. His French cologne smelled beautifully and I revelled in the sensation of his abundant chest hair tickling my so sensitive nipples. Our bodies pressed even closer together and he put his hands around my bum cheeks which pushed his huge cock against my soft tummy. At first I didn't hold it as I had no desire to appear a wanton but I could not resist letting my hand wander across the enormous shaft when his right hand slithered around from my bottom and the palm of his hand rubbed itself against my pussey, which was by now moistening like a dew-drenched flower in eager anticipation of what was to come.

'But before we proceeded any further down the path of passion, Sir Andrew Stuck showed himself to be a true aristocrat. "I would love to fuck you, dearest Gillian," he whispered quietly, "but you are only seventeen years old and may well be a virgin. I do not want you to regret this evening so even now if you decide to hold back, I will respect your wishes."

'These kind and caring words made my heart warm even more towards this considerate young man and looking steadily into his sensual dark eyes I said softly: "Andrew, I very much want you to fuck me. Yes, I am a virgin in that no cock has ever actually entered my love-tunnel, but I lost my hymen some time back thanks to all the frigging and the joys of Madame Nettleton's famous dildoes!"

'With a smile he nodded his head but still asked again: "So you are absolutely certain that you want to be fucked, Gillian?"

' "Yes, oh yes, very, very much – and right now!" I answered with some vehemence and I grasped his meaty tool, making a fist around the pulsating shaft with my fingers and I gently masturbated this tremendous love-truncheon as his fingertips slid their way into my juicy cunney. He now raised himself over me and plunged his head down to wash his tongue for a second time over my titties and I arched my back upwards as he licked so thoroughly that when I passed a hand over my tittie it felt as hard as an unripe red berry. For a split second our hot eyes locked together as I took his bursting cock in both hands and placed the purple domed helmet against the pouting cunney lips which were more than ready to receive it. He carefully inserted an inch or so of his tremendous tadger as he moved forward to lay on top of me. I spread my legs as wide as possible and wrapped my legs around his waist as our lips collided and meshed together.

'I had been concerned that I would be unable to accommodate Andrew's monster chopper but I discovered that by wriggling my bottom to and fro I could embed even more of this thick bell-end inside my cunt. As if by magic, further and further inches of pulsing prick disappeared into my creamy cunney as my pussey lips engulfed more and more of his great boner until, with a convulsive jerk of his loins, his cock was fully inserted to the very root and I cried out with glee as our bodies moved up and down in unison. What a glorious first fuck this turned out to be! How tightly my saturated slit held on to Andrew's throbbing tool! We gloried in each other's thrusts as my love juices dripped against his balls as they slapped against my bum. I implored him to drive deeper by twirling my tongue in his mouth and my buttocks rotated almost savagely in his broad palms as his lusty, gleaming joystick drove furiously into my soft depths.

' "Fill me with your spunky cream!" I urged Andrew, who for answer plunged his face between my breasts, sucking furiously at my right nipple whilst the friction in my cunney reached new heights. His wonderful prick slicked in and out of my wet crack at an even faster rate, making us both breathless with excitement. I was finding out what the glorious pleasures of a good fucking could be as my fingers now dug into the flesh of his back and my bucking torso wildly sought more and more of his magnificent prick as our pubic hairs crashed together. All the time I squirmed lasciviously and I began to shudder uncontrollably as I felt my inner depths exploding into the most delicious waves of ecstacy which bathed me in a marvellous glowing release which flowed across every fibre of my body. Each spasm racked through me and I bit poor Andrew's shoulder, which made him pump even harder. Very soon I screamed with joy as he shot powerful spurts of spunk inside my receptive cunt, his rigid prick jetting its jism into my innermost cavities with such vigour that dribblings of our mingled love juices dribbled down my thighs.

'Slowly he pulled out his gleaming penis which was still hard and when I lovingly squeezed the shaft it throbbed with latent energy. I lowered my pouting lips and flicked my pink tongue across the massive dome, juicing his shaft with my saliva as I forced the ripe plum between my lips. He trembled as I moved one hand to massage the insides of his thighs and let the other cradle his heavy, hairy ballsack. Andrew moaned as I sucked on my splendid sweetmeat, until my mouth was full and I began to move my head forwards and backwards, slurping noisily on this monster rod which tasted so tasty with that unique masculine tang. His hands clutched at my hair as I closed my lips around it as tightly as possible and worked on his knob with my tongue, easing forward gradually to take in a little more of the shaft. I circled the base with my fingers and worked my hand up and down the shaft, sucking Andrew's delicious cock until the tip almost touched the back of my throat and I cupped his balls, feeling them harden until the frothy white sperm rushed up his shaft and my mouth was filled with gorgeous gushes of sticky foam as his prick bucked wildly while I held it lightly between my teeth. I gulped down his copious emission, gratefully swallowing every last milky drop of spunk.

'Not till his delicious prick had fully shrunk back to its normal flaccidity did I withdraw my lips and then we returned to the table to partake of some more coffee which was bubbling away on a tiny gas burner and Andrew and I toasted each other before we returned to the makeshift bed where he finger-fucked me to another delicious orgasm. We finished this lewd encounter with a final *soixante-neuf* before making our way downstairs where members of Lord George Lucas's party were also set to leave.

' "Hey there, Andrew," shouted out the good-looking young son of Viscount Sevenoaks. "We're going to continue celebrating my birthday at Matthew Cosgrave's house in Grosvenor Street

– why don't you and your lovely companion join us there?" Andrew looked at me and murmured: "It's up to you, Gillian, I don't mind whether we join them or go straight back home. In all fairness, though, I must warn you that Charlie's parties have been known to, shall we say, get a little out of hand if what they tell me at the Jim Jam Club is to be believed."

' "Well, unless you are too tired, why don't we find out for ourselves?" I suggested. "We can leave at any time so long as your chauffeur is capable of getting us home."

' "Oh, there's no worry on that score, Grahame never drinks and drives," replied Andrew and so we agreed to join Lord George's gathering which was to mean, dear Rupert, that although I had only just an hour before enjoyed my very first fuck, I was now to be introduced to the wild bachannalian revels of the fastest set in London.'

At this stage she paused and giggled: 'I'll wager this lewd story has given you a big stiffie, you naughty boy.' She reached down to feel my throbbing prick which as she had correctly surmised was now at bursting point and I kissed her warm, soft lips and played with her hard titties which instantly aroused the sensuous girl.

'We need some exercise, Rupert, all this lying in bed is fine as far as it goes but we must put other muscles to use besides those in your cock and my cunney,' she said as she jumped out of bed. 'Come on, darling, you can fuck me in the Irish style, that'll be good exercise for us both.'

I looked at her with a puzzled expression until she added: 'Some people call this method "the wheelbarrow position''. Does that mean anything to you?'

'Yes, I've read about this way of fucking in *The Intimate Memoir Of Dame Jenny Everleigh* but I've never actually tried it out. Still, *experientia docet*, so if you're willing, by all means, let's see for ourselves what it's like.'

Gillian turned away from me and dropped to her hands and knees on the floor. I picked up her legs and supported much of her weight by holding her spread thighs so her arms could be fully extended and her lithe body was in a slanting position with her bottom on the same level as my cock. As soon as we were comfortable I pushed my knob forward between her bum cheeks – the only question now, as the snooker player might ask, was whether to go for the pink or the brown! I decided to slide my cock into her cunney and slipped in my length quite easily. It took a little while to achieve a satisfactory rhythm as she matched my movements with her own and I managed to 'steer' her into a position where my shaft slid very nicely in and out of her clinging sheath. I plunged in hard and in time the boiling spunk rose and, with a woosh, it surged out of my pulsating prick in a spend that seemed to last and last as I loosed a stream of sticky spunk into her dark, squelchy love-box. I withdrew and creamy drops of sperm dribbled down her thighs as I gently eased her body down onto the floor. She scrambled to her feet and kissed me, saying: 'Well, for a novice, you managed very nicely, though I must admit that I would only like to fuck this way very occasionally as it isn't the most comfortable position – it makes all the blood run into one's head.'

I was hardly surprised that Gillian was not too keen on this position for I was not that enamoured with it either – perhaps I'm old-fashioned but there's a minimum of physical contact involved and a lack of the emotional intimacy which I believe adds that little extra something to a good fucking. Mind, I'd rather take exercise in this fashion than run a mile before breakfast or in summer swim a similar distance along the River Windrush like my old pal Colonel Goldstone of the West Oxfordshire Rifles! And may I pass on a tip, dear reader, should you or your partner wish to try 'the wheelbarrow position' for yourselves? If the woman supports herself on a bed or chair, the man can place his arm round her middle and fondle her titties or pussey and she can turn her head and look at him, both of which allow a closer contact between the two of you. I find this variation preferable but as they say in that haven of devotion to the pleasures of the flesh, the Cock and Crop Club in Manhattan, 'diff'rnt strokes for diff'rnt folks'!

We climbed back into bed and Gillian lay her head on my shoulder and toyed with my still damp shaft which was in a state of half limber resting on my thigh. She said: 'I suppose you would like me to continue this tale of debauchery, wouldn't you?'

'Yes, please go on, your words are so much more interesting than anything I've heard in my lectures!'

She laughed and gave my balls a playful

squeeze. 'Very well then – where was I now? Oh yes, we followed Lord George Lucas's party back to Matthew Cosgrave's house and there must have been about a dozen or so of us in the lounge toasting the birthday boy with a jeroboam [*a huge bottle holding as much as four normal bottles – Editor*] of Mr Cosgrave's best champagne. We were all certainly a little worse for wear when one of the girls (who were all very friendly but remember, they were all from the chorus line at the Alhambra and, like most theatrical people, had few inhibitions) beckoned me to a corner where her friends had gathered.

' "We're going to give Lord George a very special birthday present," she giggled. "Do come and join the fun." She signalled to Matthew Cosgrave who called for silence and announced: "George, my dear old fellow, in honour of your birthday, we would like to present you with a little something that you'll never forget."

' "How kind of you all," murmured the dashing young peer who allowed himself to be led to a superbly made Chesterfield [*a large, tightly stuffed sofa upholstered in leather, named after the nineteenth-century Earl of Chesterfield – Editor*] in the centre of the room as Carrie, the girl who had told me about the plan, explained what she and the others – Pippa, Lucy and Suzanne – had in mind. I don't mind telling you that I was a little shocked but as I said just before, we were all quite tiddley from the champagne which was flowing like water.

'Anyhow, Lord George sat on the Chesterfield and as quick as a flash he had the four girls piled on top of him. Pippa and Lucy held down his legs whilst Carrie and Suzanne pinioned his arms, though to be truthful I can't say that our birthday boy struggled overmuch against the overpowering odds! "Gillian, I need your help," cried out Carrie, who was a real stunning girl of no more than twenty at the most blessed with an exquisitely rounded figure and an extremely pretty face with deep blue eyes set off by long dark lashes, a full mouth and a brilliant set of pearly teeth. I hurried across and took her place, holding down Lord George's left arm against the soft leather upholstery.

' "Are you going to feed him some birthday cake, girls?" laughed Roland Phillips, one of the other gay young blades who along with my escort Sir Andrew Stuck and the other men, was watching this little game unfold from the comfort of an armchair. "In good time he might be given something to eat," replied Carrie, unpinning her long tresses of light, gold-tinted auburn hair, "but first I want to find out how hungry he is." And to my astonishment she pulled open the flap of Lord George's trousers and proceeded to unbutton his flies!

' "I say, steady on, Carrie, old girl," he protested but I noticed that he did not struggle overmuch when the lovely girl tugged down his trousers and Pippa and Lucy (two lissome blonde beauties) had only to hold his legs steady whilst in one dextrous movement Carrie removed the offending garment. Along with the other girls I looked with great interest at the wisps of black pubic hair which were showing over the waistband of his drawers which had been slightly pulled down in the Mêlée and I could see his erect boner practically tearing through the fine monogrammed silk material of his aristocratic underpants! Carrie yanked these off with a whoop of joy. His rigid rod sprang up to attention and Pippa grabbed it in her fist and pumped her hand up and down with a squeal of delight.

' "Hold on there, you'll make him spend if you're not careful," warned Carrie who was now on her feet and busy unhooking her dress. "Oh, I'm terribly sorry," said Pippa, removing her hand immediately. "George, you be a good boy and wait for Carrie, do you hear?" Carrie shucked off her clothes very quickly and she flaunted her gorgeous naked body in front of us. She smoothed her hands across her magnificent swelling breasts which were round and firm and topped with large, stubby nipples. The pure whiteness of her belly was accentuated by a bushy mound of curly auburn hair through which I could just perceive the outline of her crack. Her luscious charms appealed to the other men too and I could see Roland and Andrew's trouser fronts bulge as they gawped in awe at this delicious nude apparition. But it was poor Lord George who was given the most tantalising view as Carrie began to writhe sensuously in front of him. She knelt down and let her bare breasts dangle in front of his face and then straddled him so that the tip of his straining shaft just touched her soft pussey hair. She leaned down and gave a swift series of butterfly kisses upon his blue-veined length and by now the perspiration was pouring down his forehead as he frantically tried to free himself from his captors. However, he was no match for four strapping girls and soon he was almost weeping with frustration.

' "I think he's hungry enough for you now, Carrie," smiled Suzanne and our prisoner spluttered: "Hungry enough? I'm bloody starving!"

' "Come on Carrie, it is his birthday," shouted Andrew and the gorgeous girl nodded as she climbed over George, rolling all over him and rubbing her superb titties in his face before taking hold of his enormous erection in her hand. Then she lifted herself up and sticking her bum up in the air she sat down hard on his stiffstander which slid all the way into her slit as her buttocks bounced against her thighs. She purred contentedly as she screwed herself from side to side on his bursting cock and then she began to ride her mount like a jockey on a thoroughbred. I could see his rigid rod flash in and out of her juicy cunney and then George arched his back and jetted a copious gush of spunk as she enjoyed her own climax, uninhibitedly screaming out her delight.

'She nimbly swung her legs round and jumped off her exhausted lover and Pippa piped up: "Who's next to give George a birthday present?" Andrew heaved himself up from his chair and looking at Lord George's limp prick he suggested that some girl might like to bring back this exhausted tool to life. Well, Rupert, my blood was up from watching Carrie in action and so I must admit to you that I volunteered for the job. Carrie took my place, although we hardly needed to keep hold of our victim who appeared a little *hors de combat* after his vigorous fuck, even though Carrie had done much of the work.

'I began by running my tongue along his hairy ballsack and then slowly I licked the soft length which was still wet from Carrie's spendings. This soon had the desired effect and his prick gradually swelled up until I found it difficult to accommodate its throbbing thickness between my lips. So I went back to his scrotum and kissed his sweet nuts whilst I gently rubbed his strong, sinewy shaft with my hand. I took my time and his cock and balls received a prolonged salivating which made him groan in ecstacy. When I had sucked up his sabre-curved cock to its fullest erection, I reached behind him and inserted a moistened fingertip into his bottom hole. With my other hand I cupped his tightening ballsack and set up a rhythmic motion, bobbing my head up and down in time with my finger. As I now know, there is not a man in the whole wide world who can resist a good gobble and I only had to squeeze his balls two or three times before he rolled his hips and sent thick wads of creamy, hot spunk down my throat. To the applause of the other guests, I eagerly swallowed his spend which tasted slightly sweeter than Andrew's sperm.'

'Did you then let him fuck your dear little cunt?' I asked breathlessly, reaching down to stroke her damp pussey.

'Certainly not,' she retorted sharply, 'don't forget it was only an hour or two earlier that evening I had first had any prick penetrate my pussey. If I was to be fucked again, it would only be by Andrew Stuck, the man who had so carefully and considerately taken my unwanted virginity.'

I apologised profusely for my hasty remark which Gillian gracefully accepted in the nicest way possible – by opening her legs and letting me rub her dampening slit whilst she took hold of my burgeoning boner and the next thing I knew I was looking down at her and my sturdy prick was being guided between Gillian's welcoming pussey lips. She whimpered and closed her legs around my waist to hold me tight as she began that rapid rippling contraction of her cunney muscles which so excited me. This was to be no slow, lingering fuck for we were both urgent in our needs and as I thrust into her again and again she rose to meet me with equal vigour. Great gasps swept through our bodies and she cried out: 'Rupert, Rupert, I'm spending, you big cocked boy! I'm spending, shoot your spunk inside me!'.

It was an easy command to obey for already I could feel the first spurt of milky cream forcing its way along my pulsing prick. This was shortly followed by another as I discharged a powerful stream of sperm and Gillian's own juices flowed liberally in response. She seized tight hold of me and we fucked away quite uncontrollably, writhing and twisting on the bed until we were both totally drained. As we lay there entwined in each other's arms, panting and sucking in great gulps of air, we were so overcome that neither of us could speak for a while as we shared our post-fuck fatigue.

Gillian was the first to recover her senses and she said: 'What a simply marvellous bout of love-making. I came at least three times, Rupert, you have such a clever cock.'

'Thank you very much,' I said modestly, though like all men I was delighted to be complimented upon my performance. 'But any credit must be equally shared with your divine cunney and I suppose the wonderfully lewd account of your rite of passage also helped stir my imagination.'

She smiled and continued: 'Oh, I am pleased you enjoyed it. Don't think too badly of me because I sucked Lord George Lucas's cock after Sir Andrew Stuck had fucked me.'

'Good grief, of course not, Gillian, why, so long as you had no objection I must confess here and now that if a lovely girl came into the room and asked me to fuck her, I would have no compunction about obliging her.'

'Really, Rupert? You are not just saying that to make me feel less guilty after telling you how free I was with my favours that night?'

'No, honestly, darling, I'm doing nothing of the kind,' I assured her in all truthfulness, though I wondered why she wanted to lead the conversation in this very personal direction. 'Why on earth shouldn't a girl let herself go once in a while just in the same way a man can without being labelled as anything but a chip off the old block.'

'Why indeed, Rupert, but there is such an overwhelming prejudice against women enjoying themselves in bed that even though I surmised you were not so blockheadedly chauvinistic about this matter, I wanted to make sure before imparting any information about a party being held at the aptly named Oxford Playhouse on Saturday night. I've been invited and told I may bring a friend but I didn't want to mention anything to you until I was sure that you wouldn't be stuffy about it.'

'Who's throwing the party? Is it town or gown?' I asked, more than a mite puzzled by this little speech.

She smiled and replied: 'Neither really, my love, it's for the cast of *A Nice Little Stroll Does You Good* which has been running at the theatre for the last two weeks before it transfers to Birmingham and then on to the Holborn Empire in London. The show is one of Mrs Susan Moser's lush musical comedies and the impresario, Mr Louis Segal, is so pleased with the reviews it's attracted in the provincial papers so far that he is putting on this party for the cast and some friends. You might know that he often tries out his productions in out of town theatres before spending a lot of money putting on a show in the West End.

'But you see, I've been invited because one of Sir Andrew Stuck's hobbies is to invest in theatrical productions, and he is one of the major backers of *A Nice Little Stroll Does You Good*, and all four of the girls who were at Lord George Lucas's birthday party are in the chorus and naturally they will also be at the party. But if their presence or Andrew being there would bother you, then I'm quite happy to go on my own.'

'For heaven's sake, that won't be necessary,

you silly goose. We are both free agents and can live our lives as we alone wish to live them.'

She puckered up her lips and planted a kiss on my cheek. As she snuggled up to me I felt her relax, but moments later we were disturbed by a soft knocking on the door.

'Who is it?' asked Gillian with an unconcerned yawn.

'It's Chrissie,' came the whispered reply. 'May I come in, please?'

I looked questioningly at Gillian's naked body. 'Hadn't we better make ourselves decent?'

'There is no need, Chrissie is a very close friend and to be frank I've discovered her in a similar position more than once so it hardly matters one way or the other if she now sees me in a state of undress in bed with my lover.'

'Come in, Chrissie,' she called out and the door opened to reveal a tall, dark-haired girl dressed in a short tennis dress. Her willowy figure was capped by an attractively pert face with bright brown eyes which matched her long tresses of soft hair falling down in ringlets to her shoulders. 'Chrissie, meet Rupert Mountjoy; Rupert, this is Miss Chrissie Nayland-Hunt, one of the three girls who shares this house with me.'

I heaved myself to a more upright position, but our visitor said with a twinkle in her eye: 'A pleasure to meet you, Rupert. Please don't get up, it looks as if you have had a tiring afternoon.'

'He has performed splendidly, Chrissie, and it is truly a serendipitous coincidence that you have joined us at this time. We were just discussing some intimate matters and I don't think it's more

116

than five minutes ago that Rupert declared that so long as I have no objection – and I have none as far as you are concerned – he would happily oblige any pretty girl who desired the thrill of his stiff cock in her cunney.'

'Is this true, Rupert?' enquired this scrumptious lass as she came in and sat on the bed. 'Let me see for myself what exactly you have to offer.' And before I could say or do anything more she pulled the covers off my side of the bed and exposed my dormant but still swollen shaft which was in a state of half limber.

She took hold of my prick and commented: 'Gillian, you must have really extracted great pleasure from this fine instrument.'

'I have indeed, Chrissie, along with a copious amount of hot, frothy, masculine seed,' agreed my pretty bedmate. 'Would you care to take your pleasure with Rupert? He is a true gentleman and though his cock must be somewhat fatigued after our strenuous exertions, I am sure that with a little assistance this fine organ will be capable of rising to the occasion.'

Perhaps I should have been angered by Gillian's cool suggestion to her friend which took no account of *my* feelings about whether or not I wanted to fuck Chrissie, though to be fair I had been hoist by my own petard through my rash remark about happily obliging any girl etc, etc, the words of which Gillian had glibly repeated to the newcomer. Anyhow, Chrissie looked simply ravishing in her skimpy white tennis dress which set off her long dark tresses and large brown eyes and only a confirmed homosexualist would have failed to have been aroused by her sensuous pulchritude.

So I raised no objection when Chrissie leaned forward and proceeded to take my penis in her smooth, soft hands, resting her forearms on my belly and thighs. As Gillian had forecast, it needed little further encouragement for it immediately began to swell to its fullest extent under her warm touch. She cupped my ballsack in one hand and lightly ran the fingers of the other along the bright blue veins of my distended love truncheon.

'Master John Thomas looks to be well on the road to recovery, but to make sure I'd best give him the kiss of life,' she murmured and I gave a huge grin of approval as she leaned forward and took my throbbing tool between her ruby lips, teasing my knob against the roof of her mouth. Ripples of ecstacy flowed out from my delighted stiffstander as her darting tongue moved to and fro along the thick shaft and I closed my eyes and lay back, totally engulfed in the exquisite sensations which were now washing all over my body.

Frankly, I sometimes wonder whether being sucked off isn't even more pleasurable than actually fucking though I suppose it depends upon one's mood and the skills of one's partner. Certainly Chrissie was a fellatrix *par excellence* and as she licked the tip of my cock I felt my balls begin to tighten and fill with jism. Chrissie sensed this and for a moment took her sweet lips away. Then with a wicked smile she returned to the fray, stroking her tongue along the underside of my cock, making it ache with excitement as I jerked my body upwards and thrust frenziedly into her oral orifice. She squeezed her hand around the base of my prick, sucking it even harder and this exquisite sensation sent me to paradise. But I could contain myself for only a short while longer and I let out a short, sharp cry of despair as my lusty young prick pulsed in her mouth and I jetted spurt after spurt of creamy white semen full into her adorable mouth. She managed to suck in and swallow every last drop of my libation, licking all round my knob to take up the final sticky dribbles of jism.

She raised her head and looking me squarely in the eye said mischievously: 'Well, that was a truly delicious *hors d'oeuvre*, Rupert, but now how about the main course? I'm glad to see that your cock's still quite hard, can you keep it up whilst I undress?'

'I'll help to keep his organ on song,' said Gillian brightly, taking hold of my moist length and rubbing it gaily between her hands. This had the desired effect of keeping my shaft stiff as Chrissie slipped out of her clothes. For a girl with such a slim, almost boyish figure, Chrissie had a surprisingly full bosom with rounded, firmly shaped breasts tipped with pert raspberry nipples surrounded by large red aureolae. I watched closely as she ran her hands along the smooth skin of her flat, unwrinkled belly and into a luxuriant fleece of dark, almost black hair which extended between her thighs and completely covered her pussey. She leaped into bed beside me and straightaway took a pillow and placed it under her bottom as she spread her legs to wait for the arrival of my twitching tool which under Gillian's continuing rhythmic ministrations was now standing proudly upright in all its glory, the purple helmet uncapped and glowing as she worked my shaft up and down in her hands.

'Chrissie, are you ready to receive His Majesty, King Cock?' she gaily enquired.

The darling girl replied: 'Yes, dear, please put Rupert's tool in my cunt, I have a great fancy for it just now. I want to feel his knob nudge between my pussey lips and drive straight through into my cunney.'

Gillian moved a hand across to delve into Chrissie's thick growth of pubic hair. Her clever fingers spread her friend's pussey lips and exposed the pink chink where my pulsating prick was now yearning to enter. With Gillian's hand still firmly clasped on my tadger, I rolled over on top of the trembling girl and she opened the lips of Chrissie's cunt and placed the tip of my helmet between them. 'Push on, Rupert,' she hissed in my ear. 'Chrissie has a marvellously tight little cunney and she wants to feel every inch of your big cock inside her!'

I needed no further urging and planting my lips on hers, I plunged forward, embedding my knob and just an inch or so of my shaft inside her delicious, velvet-walled cunt. Quickly, we established a fine rhythm with Chrissie pushing her hips upward to meet every push forward of my prick into her already sopping cunney. We enjoyed an excellent fuck (though is there such a thing as a bad one!) with her rapid jerking spurring me to further fast plunges into this delectable cunt which held my member in its warm, silky embrace. Her juices lubricated her little love-channel so that my cock slid in and out of her pussey with consummate ease though it was tight enough for me to feel my foreskin being drawn backwards and forwards with every lascivious shove. I fucked away with surprising energy considering how Gillian had emptied my balls before Chrissie had sucked me off just before. But the throbbing contractions of her cunney muscles spurred me on and we shared a truly memorable experience.

'Ah, you lovely boy, ram home that fat joystick!' she urged me as her eyes sparkled and she writhed in delicious agitations as within us the pent-up waves of ecstatic bliss rose to tidal proportions. A few more rapid, impetuous thrusts together with one last straining of her body to mine and her fingers clawed up and down my back as she reached the highest pinnacle of pleasure. Very shortly afterwards I joined her and I spouted a stream of milky seed inside Chrissie's cunney which mingled deliciously with her own copious rivulets of nectar that overflowed down onto her thighs. I pounded my spurting shaft until I was spent and I collapsed on top of her soft body, and the two of us were almost fainting with fatigue after this torrid fuck.

Both Chrissie and I had been so highly involved with each other's bodies that neither of us had noticed Gillian slip out of bed whilst we had been fucking ourselves into a stupor. But the kind girl had busied herself whilst my love trunk was battering its way into Chrissie's cunt and she had set up a table upon which she had placed a selection of fruits and a jug of lemonade from the ice-box. The clever girl knew full well that a prolonged bout of fucking uses a great deal of energy and that even our strong, youthful bodies required refreshment to regain our strength. We were so warm from our fun and games that we stayed quite naked as we enjoyed our informal tea, during which I asked Chrissie what she was studying at Oxford.

'I'm reading for a degree in the history of art,' she explained as she sat up in bed munching an apple, 'and as I enjoy painting, for my own amusement, I am also studying watercolour techniques in an informal weekly class under the tuition of Professor Tim Titchfield of All Souls, who offers his kind guidance to any budding artists among the first year students.'

Now I had dabbled a little in painting since my first encounter with art which had led directly to my crossing the Rubicon with the divine Diana Wigmore [see An Edwardian Dandy 1: Youthful Scandals – Editor] that in turn had given me the unexpected but highly delightful chance to lose my unwanted virginity. Sadly, my efforts with the brush and palette were so far undistinguished, though I was told by Diana that I would do far better once I had been taught to harness my technical skills to create my own personal style.

So I asked Chrissie if any student could avail himself of Professor Titchfield's classes. 'Most certainly,' she replied. 'Why, would you like to come along? We meet on Thursday evenings at eight o'clock in the small lecture hall just next to the Playhouse Theatre.'

'I'll be there,' I promised and, turning to Gillian, I said: 'Talking of the Playhouse, will Chrissie be invited to this party on Saturday night? I'm sure you could wangle her onto the guest list.'

'Of course, but unless I'm much mistaken, she'll be wining and dining with her new special boyfriend who's coming all the way over from Cambridge for the weekend just to be with her.'

Chrissie blushed and said: 'Now you know full well, Gillian, that Salman is just a boyfriend, and there is nothing special about him – except of course that he is a very charming young man—'

'– who has pots and pots of money and a very, very big cock!' finished Gillian with a giggle.

'Wash your mouth out, you bad girl!' scolded Chrissie although she was not really offended by the jest. 'Salman's cock is certainly sizeable but it is not the very biggest I have ever entertained in my pussey. That honour would go to "Donkey Dick" Dinchley, the gardener's boy at my Uncle Rodney's country house in Buckinghamshire whose erect tool measured almost twelve and a half inches, though he was by no means the most satisfying fuck. I mean, we both had that good-looking chap Harry Barr at your birthday party in May and he was superb in bed even though his member was if anything smaller than the average cock. Don't you agree that this obsession with the size of their penises makes many men almost neurotic? And it's all so unnecessary because as an American girl in my college says, it isn't the size of the ship that counts, it's the motion of the ocean!'

'Yes, although I suppose it is a similar problem

that we women have in never being quite satisfied with our weight!' said Gillian thoughtfully, but before she could continue airing her views on this admittedly interesting subject, I suddenly woke up to the fact that Chrissie's boyfriend could be none other than my old school chum Salman Marrari, the eldest son of the Maharajah of Lockshenstan who had, as I noted at the very beginning of these memoirs, spurned a place at University College, Oxford to take up a place at Trinity College, Cambridge as he wanted to continue his scientific studies with some noted group of physicists who were based there. He was also a great cocksman and very popular with the servant girls at St Lionel's amongst whom he distributed a generous number of twenty pound notes for favours great and small!

So I asked her excitedly: 'Are you talking about Salman Marrari who went up to Cambridge from St Lionel's? He shared a study with me at school and it would be marvellous to see him if he is coming to Oxford this weekend. Is this the chap who you are seeing, Chrissie?'

'Yes indeed, what a lovely coincidence,' she said, clapping her hands together. 'Oh, Rupert, you must join us for dinner on Friday night.'

'That's very kind but surely you two prefer to dine *à deux*.'

'No, really, you must come along – I won't tell Salman so it will be a lovely surprise for him to see his old school chum again,' she insisted.

It was time for us to take our leave but Chrissie assured me that she would send round a note about where I should meet her and Salman on

Friday night. After kissing the two girls goodbye I walked back briskly to my college, making a mental note as I looked at my watch that I would need to employ a social secretary if invitations were to keep flowing so freely into my diary. When I reached my rooms I jotted down my immediate engagements – this evening I had planned to see Beth Randall after dinner and take her for a walk and perhaps visit one of the quaint old Oxford inns frequented (though much frowned upon) by students of the University. Tomorrow I had to attend two lectures and write a long essay which had to be given in the next morning, but time would be at a premium as I had already accepted Professor Webb's invitation to his soirée. I had some reading to do as well but the weekend was already filling up for on Friday I was to dine with Salman and Chrissie, whilst on Saturday night I would squire Gillian to the party at the Oxford Playhouse. I gnawed my lip in a gesture of irritation as I suddenly remembered that on Saturday afternoon I was due to play soccer for Balliol against Merton College and I really should fit in at least a couple of hours of training before the match. Of course, I could always cut a lecture or two, but at his specific request, I had promised my godfather, Major Fulham, that I would never allow this to happen during my first year and since my earliest years I have always maintained that a promise is a promise – and especially when you have just been handed a cheque for fifty pounds 'to be spent on enjoying yourself, my boy; your father can look after the college fees and your account at Blackwell's bookshop'!

This left Sunday as the only day free to work and though my family have never been strict observers of the Sabbath, I knew full well that if the Saturday party turned out to be the kind of affair I hopefully expected, I would be in no fit state to study the day afterwards! Still, these were pleasant problems to solve and I resolved to lighten my load by postponing my tryst with Beth until the following week and instead making a start on my essay after dinner, even though Frank and Barry would do their best to inveigle me into playing a few rubbers of bridge. I would be very tempted as I much enjoyed the game, but however hard it would be, their blandishments would have to be resisted, I said to myself as I made my way downstairs to spend half an hour reading the newspapers in the library before going into the dining hall.

In the library I picked up a copy of *The Times* and coincidentally one of the first reports to catch my eye was a review of *A Nice Little Stroll Does You Good*. Under the heading 'A Jolly Evening Well Spent' the critic had written: 'As several friends in the profession have told me about the rousing reception *A Nice Little Stroll Does You Good* has been given in the provincial theatres before opening in two weeks' time in London, I ventured out to Oxford to see Mr Louis Segal's latest musical comedy for myself, and am pleased to report that this latest offering is about as good and as clever as any play in this genre. The songs are jolly and the story, though of the sort we have seen more often than not, is at least well paced and, though relying on mishaps and misunderstandings for its dramatic effects, all ends happily with the hero and heroine reaping their rewards and the villains getting their just deserts. It is conceived as a downright, rollicking, noisy comedy and the humour and praiseworthy characterisations evinced by the principals, Mr Michael Bailey, Mr Frederick Shackleton and Miss Deborah Paxford undoubtedly caught the imagination of the audience. They are abetted by one of the prettiest chorus lines, whose shapely forms are clothed perhaps in too scanty a fashion for the older generation, but all can act and sing as well as they can dance. From first to last, all on stage appear to revel in the fun and the company complied with repeated requests for encores without displaying any symptom of weariness.'

Then and there I decided to check with Gillian as to whether she already possessed tickets for Saturday night, because after such a review the playgoers of Oxford and the surrounding villages would flock to see the show. I scribbled a note and found a young college servant who for sixpence was willing to deliver the message that evening and (so long as Gillian was at home) wait and bring back her reply.

The gong sounded as I gave the lad my note and made him repeat the address I had just given him (for the matter was important and I did not want my note to go astray) and Frank Folkestone ambled up and accompanied me into the dining-hall. 'Hello there, old boy, I haven't seen much of you since Len Letchmore regaled us with his lewd tale about his uncle and the chorus girl.

'Talking of chorus girls,' he added, 'how about

127

coming along with me to see the show at the Playhouse one night? I've spoken to a few chaps who have already seen it and they all say that it's great fun with some cracking chorus girls. Do you know that Malcolm Ross, the fellow from Winchester who rowed for Oxford in the Boat Race this year – well, he went backstage with a bunch of flowers and a note for one of the girls and she accepted his invitation to dine at Carlo's Restaurant after the performance the following evening.'

'You think she sang for her supper?' I said with a grin.

'I don't honestly know, but the newspapers say the chorus line is well worth watching especially as some of the costumes are rather naughty,' said Frank with undisguised relish. 'So how about it, old boy?'

Trying hard not to sound conceited, I explained to Frank (and to Barry Jacobs who had just joined us) that I already had an invitation to meet the cast on Saturday night at a private party after the show, but that if I could smuggle my pals in, I'd let them know as soon as possible. 'Gosh, you're a fast worker, Rupert,' said Frank admiringly. 'Talk about being quick off the mark. If this gathering is anything like the theatrical revels I've read about in the *Jenny Everleigh* books, it's just as well you're playing football before and not after the party!'

'Yes, especially as I'm playing with you in the team on Saturday afternoon and Esme Dyotte is coming to watch the game. I want to be on the winning side, Rupert, so be a good chap and keep your mind off your cock and on the match until we've beaten Merton by at least six goals!'

Frank shook his head in warning. 'You'll be lucky if you manage to scrape a draw, Barry. Merton plan to field four Corinthians [*a famous English amateur football club in the early years of the century whose members were mostly drawn from the top public schools and that often played matches against leading professional sides – Editor*] in their line-up.'

'Gosh, we'll have a real fight on our hands,' said Barry gloomily. 'It jolly well serves me right for wanting to show off in front of Esme.'

'Cheer up, old lad – at least you aren't playing in goal so she won't have to see you bending down every ten minutes to pick the ball out of the net,' said Frank, though perhaps not surprisingly these words of comfort elicited only a glare from Barry.

'I think I'll take up golf instead,' he muttered. 'At least I can only let myself down on the course. Still, I'm sure that win or lose Esme will keep to our arrangement on Sunday. She can't see me after the match because she's going with your friend Beth Randall to see *The Taming Of The Shrew* at the New Theatre on Saturday night along with some other girls. But I'm planning to take her out to Standlake for luncheon on Sunday.'

'I didn't know there were any public houses serving meals on Sunday round there, though it's a pretty part of the county,' I commented.

'You're right, Rupert, there aren't any but Mr and Mrs Greenacre, some old friends of my parents, live there and yesterday Mr Greenacre called and asked me to join them for lunch on Sunday. He said that I should bring a friend if I would like to, so I've asked Esme.'

'And has she accepted?' asked Frank.

'I'm waiting for her reply as I only left a message at her rooms this morning. I wrote to her after what happened at Doctor Blayers' party, and I do hope that she will come to Standlake with me. To be frank, I'm a bit worried as I went over the top a bit when I wrote to her.'

'Oh, don't worry at all about that,' I said with all the assurance of an eighteen-year-old man of the world. 'I don't think you can over-flatter a woman. Remember what Ovid said: *Quae dant, quaeque negant, gaudent tamen esse roatae.*'

'Whether they give or refuse, women are pleased to have been asked,' translated Frank and Barry's face brightened.

'You think so?' he said as we stood up to greet the dons who marched their way through to the High Table. 'I wrote her a little poem,' he added as we resumed our seats. 'Would you like to hear it?'

'Why not?' said Frank and as Nancy (of all people!) plonked brimming plates of oxtail soup in front of us Barry fumbled in his pocket and brought out a piece of paper and began to read his Ode to Esme:

'I care not what other men may say,
The maid that suits my mind,
Is the girl who meets me on the way
And while she is free, she is kind.
With her beauties never could I be cloyed
Such pleasures I find by her side;
I don't love her less because she's enjoyed
By many another beside.

> *She opens her thighs without fear or dread,*
> *And points to her dear little crack,*
> *Its lips are so red, and all overspread*
> *With hair of the glossiest black.*
> *Reclined on her breasts or clasped in her arms,*
> *With her my best moments I spend,*
> *And revel the more in her sweet melting charms,*
> *Because they are shared with a friend.'*

'A splendid effort, old chum,' I said, although I wondered how Esme would take to Barry's emphasis on the fact that Beth and I had also romped with her during that wild night at The Cat and Pigeons hotel.

Frank also congratulated the poet and Nancy whispered a 'well done' in Barry's ear as she waited for us to finish our soup.

The fish course was a rather undistinguished piece of grilled cod but when this had been cleared away Nancy brought a fine roast joint of beef to the table and placed it before me to carve for the eight of us who were sitting at our table.

My father had taught me to carve at an early age so I had no worries as I rose, knife and fork in hand, to make the first incision into the mouthwatering piece of beef in front of me. But as I looked up the table to the students furthest away from me and asked whether they preferred their meat rare or well-done, I was startled by what appeared to be a small hand grabbing my ankle underneath the table. I cast a glance down but could see nothing as the overhanging white tablecloth concealed all. Saying nothing except to enquire as to how the other diners wished to have their beef prepared, I manfully carried on carving as the mysterious but determined hand started to stroke first my ankle and then the upper part of my calf.

I wondered whether it was Nancy playing a practical joke and looked around for her, but she was nowhere to be seen and another maid brought bowls of roast potatoes and green vegetables to our table. Now I enjoy a good joke as much as the next man but there was a time and place for this admittedly agreeable massage. However, right now I wanted to tuck in to my dinner so I simply ignored the wandering fingers which by now had reached my knees. What should I do? I had no wish to call over a steward for certainly poor Nancy would face instant dismissal without a reference. So I just sat down and savoured the first delicious mouthful as Nancy's hand moved speedily along my thigh and reached into my lap. There it thankfully rested for a moment as Humphrey Price, the broad-shouldered captain of our football team, called across from an adjoining table: 'Rupert, I hope you will be able to score goals on Saturday afternoon with the same facility as the way you carved that hunk of beef.'

'I'll do my best, Humphrey,' I responded as burrowing beneath my napkin, Nancy's hand felt for and grasped my cock. Now in normal circumstances, such behaviour would have caused Mr Priapus to swell up in greeting but even when she undid my fly buttons, my prick stayed quiescent – but when she slid her hand inside my drawers and started to caress my naked shaft it now began to stir perceptibly with a swelling excitement, especially when she pulled back my foreskin and washed the exposed smooth-skinned knob with long, lingering licks of her tongue as she coaxed my shaft up into life by sliding her hand up and down its expanding length.

Nevertheless, I was determined not to allow this strange turn of events get out of hand, but the mundane task of passing the salt to Frank Folkestone almost shattered my mask of calm as Nancy's hand had now won the battle and my prick stood high, erect and throbbing. Her firm fingers now pulled it towards her soft lips which kissed my knob lightly before opening wide to admit my twitching tool inside the deliciously wet cavern of her mouth. I took my glass and swallowed down a draught of wine as, drawing a deep breath and making a supreme effort to relax, I impaled a piece of beef on my fork. At the same time, inch by inch, Nancy was fucking my cock with her mouth, bobbing her head backwards and forwards as I chewed on the equally tender food on my plate. For a short while I managed to continue eating without showing any outward signs of agitation but soon I became aware of the first rising spasm of sperm starting its journey up from my balls and along my distended staff. I tried to hold back but the insistent pressure from Nancy's lashing tongue was too much and with an involuntary jerk of my hips, I sent a stream of hot spunk crashing into her mouth. This sudden movement caused me to choke on a barely chewed wedge of cabbage as the wicked girl gobbled furiously on my spurting prick.

Barry Jacobs shifted his chair to move closer to me and slapped me on the back. 'Are you all right, Rupert?' he asked anxiously. 'Has something gone down the wrong way?'

'Not exactly,' I spluttered, drawing in fresh gulps of air whilst Nancy hungrily continued to suck and swallow the last drains of spunk from my now thankfully deflating shaft. 'I'll be all right once everything has gone down.' I could have sworn that I heard Nancy giggle at this and I looked around sharply but fortunately no-one else had heard her. As we finished our main course I deliberately dropped a spoon on to the floor and bent down ostensibly to pick it up but in reality to catch a glimpse of the tousled mop of hair still nestling between my thighs. Nancy looked up at me and winked as she gave my flaccid cock a final lick before pulling her head away, which allowed me to hastily button up my gaping flies.

The plates were now cleared away and Frank said: 'There's apple and blackberry tart to follow, gentlemen, the perfect finish to an old-fashioned English dinner, don't you think?'

As I nodded my agreement, however, I noticed with a smile that another diner at our table, a jolly, gregarious Scot from Stirlingshire named Michael Beattie who had this evening donned his traditional Scottish dress, was sitting bolt upright in his chair with a startled expression on his face. One didn't need to be the winner of a scholarship to guess that Nancy had lifted his kilt and in her own inimitable way was cementing the Act of

Union! Wicked though it was, I just could not restrain myself from leaning forward and asking Michael (who was a great theatregoer and a leading light in the Oxford University Dramatic Society [OUDS]) whether he planned to see the show at the Playhouse this week. 'There are supposed to be some sparkling songs which could be considered for the Christmas revue.

'And you could always use some new jokes, couldn't you? I mean, we all know the good old stories from the music hall like the girl asking you what's worn under the kilt and your answer being, nothing's worn, Miss Jones, everything is in perfect working order,' I added mischievously.

He seemed unable to reply but instead threw me a glassy smile and I surmised that Nancy had now taken his claymore out of its scabbard and was, so to speak, busy Tossing the Caber. It would have been cruel to carry on teasing poor Michael but so not to arouse suspicion, I steered the conversation along a tangent to the Dramatic Society's current presentation of *The Taming Of The Shrew*, of which Michael was the stage manager. 'But we mustn't neglect the OUDS offering at the New Theatre,' I said, turning to the other side of the table. 'Everyone who has seen the play has praised the production to the skies, not least the performance of Lily Brayton in the title role. I would imagine that our amateur players must have been in awe at treading the boards with such a distinguished Shakespearean actress. *[Professional actresses playing female roles in OUDS productions was a well-established tradition until the nineteen-twenties, when there were enough female undergraduates available for selection by the Dramatic Society. Miss Lily Brayton, who Rupert mentions here, was indeed an accomplished actress who had played Katharine in a West End production the previous year — Editor].*

'You went to see the play last night, Roger,' I said to the Honourable Roger Tagholm, the younger son of Viscount Bloomsbury and a polite young man who was sitting across from Michael Beattie, whose face was now screwed up in a contortion which suggested he was suffering from indigestion though I speculated that Nancy was about to draw a large dram of Highland Cream from Michael's Caledonian cock. 'Tell us frankly whether you enjoyed it. Michael and his friends would want your honest opinion on the matter.'

'I enjoyed it very much and that's a fact,' said Roger warmly. 'Lily Brayton plays her part as Katharine so well that I could believe she is a real shrew off the stage as well as on it, though I'm sure that is not really the case at all. She brought out the best in Fred Newman who I think hit on the right method of playing his difficult role. Petruchio is after all a gentleman who pretends to be a ruffian and Fred realised this, blustering through his lines as a noisy bully yet showing that he is only acting the part, yet not so clearly that Katharine will see through the pretence. I also thought the quieter scenes between Bianca and Vincentio were very well played by Gwendolen Bunbury and Arthur Cuthbertson, who made a very handsome couple indeed.'

This generous critique was interrupted by a

long drawn-out sigh of release from Michael Beattie whose balls had obviously been relieved of a copious discharge of *uisge beatha* via Nancy's unseen palating of his prick under the table. 'I'm so pleased you enjoyed the play,' he said, his voice croaking with emotion which the others may have believed was brought on by Roger's praise but which I guessed was caused by Nancy nipping his sticky knob with her teeth as she licked up the remains of his spend, 'and I'm especially glad that you thought Gwendolen and Arthur played their love scenes so convincingly, as they had a little problem last night and I had a hand in solving it.'

But when we pressed him to say more he declined and we rose to take our coffee outside the dining-hall. Nevertheless, after Frank, Barry and myself had settled down with Michael in a quiet corner of the large, high-ceilinged common-room, we asked him again to enlarge upon his curious remark. At first he declined but then his face crinkled into a broad grin and he said: 'Look, if you will all promise me faithfully that none of you will spread this story to anyone else, I'll tell you what actually happened backstage last night between Gwen and Arthur because looking back, it was really rather funny – though I didn't find it all that amusing at the time!'

'Of course, we promise that we won't tell a soul,' we chorused and it is only now, some years after the events here described took place and after I have received the written permission to record the facts of the matter from both Arthur and Gwendolen (now Lady Royce-Mainwaring), that I am setting down Michael's secret story for a far wider audience than when it was first recounted to me.

'All right then,' said Michael, as we took up Barry's usual generous offer to buy a bottle of port for the table. 'I'll start at the beginning. Perhaps you won't be surprised to learn that since women have been allowed to join OUDS there has been a marked increase in the number of fellows willing not just to tread the boards but to take on such work as set construction, scene-shifting, prompting and all the many other jobs necessary to mount a successful production. After all, you might not be paid for your time but there's usually a good chance of meeting any number of pretty girls during the rehearsals, and afterwards, when we invariably go out for a drink, there's usually time to try and form a closer relationship. And working backstage, especially when you're putting on a historical play, there are often several quick changes of costume to be made, and I've never found it a bother to help scantily dressed girls to change into their clothes.

'Now it was clear to all of us involved in putting on *The Taming Of The Shrew* that Arthur and Gwendolen were clearly enjoying their love scenes on stage – so much so in fact that during the dress rehearsal, after a farewell kiss lasted more than a minute, the director, Sidney Smyth, had to shout out: "Hey, that's enough, you two, this is Shakespeare not a Victor Pudendum show at the Jim Jam Club!"

'This admonition worked only as far as the first night and since then their on-stage kisses have been becoming longer and longer and a few days ago Sidney Smyth threatened to throw a bucket of water over them if they embraced for longer than ten seconds! Well, last night he deputed me to ensure that Gwendolen and Arthur behaved themselves. Now there is a thirty-five minute break between when the pair leave the stage to when they have to make their next entrance so I thought I would keep a close eye on them during this interval.

'I made my way to Gwendolen's dressing room, which was at the far end of a small, badly lit corridor. There was a light shining through the door which was only slightly ajar and I could hear the soft murmur of voices as I approached. As I had guessed, Gwen was talking to Arthur, but I was shocked and faced with a difficult dilemma when I heard her whisper throatily: "Suck my titties, darling, you know how that excites me!" Should I or should I not make my presence known and break up their spooning? I peered in through the gap left by the half-shut door. Gwendolen looked simply stunning – if you've never met her, let me tell you that she is a most attractive girl, well-built with long curly strawberry-blonde hair and a curvey figure. She had taken off the dress she was wearing in Act One and was lying in Arthur's arms on a pile of clothes heaped on the floor wearing only a silk camisole which had ridden up to reveal her frilly white knickers. She had let the shoulder straps fall down and Arthur had cupped her large creamy white breasts in his hands. He had taken off his shirt and vest but had kept on his tights which bulged so much between his legs I thought that the material would soon give way! Gwendolen stroked this enormous bulge as she repeated her request for Arthur to suck her titties. She made herself comfortable on his lap, put her arm around his neck and pulled his face to her naked nipples.

' "Oooh! Oooh! How lovely," she moaned as he nibbled gently away, tweaking one erect red tittie between the fingers of his left hand as he twisted his tongue around the other, and Gwendolen moaned with delight, holding him in a vicelike grip as with his right hand he lifted her camisole even higher to rub his palm against her pussey. She arched her back upwards to allow him to pull down her knickers and I don't mind telling you that this sight made my own cock swell up so much that I was forced to unbutton my flies and let my stiff shaft spring out of my trousers. My hand flew to my rigid rod but somehow I managed to resist the temptation to toss myself off. Instead, I squeezed my bursting prick as I watched Arthur's fingers burying themselves in Gwendolen's furry mound, which made her shake in a series of spasms before she gasped: "Arthur, let me do something for you." He pulled away for a moment and attempted to take off his tights. He pushed them over the protuberance made by his swollen prick and let them down together with his underpants down to his ankles.

'Gwendolen reached out and grasped his tumescent tool, sliding her hand up and down the thick veiny shaft and they frigged each other frenziedly as they exchanged a long, deep French kiss. I could no longer contain myself and indulged in a rapid five knuckle shuffle. Gwendolen lay back and spread her legs and the sight of Arthur's fingers sliding in and out of her hairy crack brought me to the boil very quickly and turning aside I ejaculated a stream of creamy jism all over the wall behind me. In double quick time I mopped it up with a handkerchief as best as I could. Then as I dried my knob I looked back again at the frenetic couple in the room in front of me who by now were about to progress to an actual fuck. Gwendolen was now on her back with her head resting on a plump cushion and Arthur was on his knees between her legs. He grabbed a second cushion and slid it under her backside and then he nudged her knees further apart as he took his thick prick in his hand and carefully inserted the uncapped bulbous helmet into her cunney. I swear I could hear the squelchy sound of his shaft parting her love lips and entering her cunt as she clasped her legs around his waist and he fucked her in a slow yet steady rhythm, his hands cupping her breasts as he pumped in and out of her juicy love channel.

' "Go on big boy, fuck my pussey with that big fat dick. Ram your cock into my crack you dear lad!" she cried out as she drummed her feet against the small of his back to force every inch of his pulsating tool inside her. Arthur was now panting from his exertions as he pounded away, his body rocking backwards and forwards between her spread fleshy thighs. Gwendolen was obviously spending as she raked his back with her fingernails as she thrilled to the sweet sensations of her spend, but as he trembled on the brink of his climax she gasped: "Best not come inside me tonight, Arthur, it's not a good time of the month." "Oh, damnation!" he grunted, clearly disappointed but gallantly and wisely, he jerked his hips upward and withdrawing his gleaming, throbbing penis, proceeded to shoot a flood of milky white semen all over her belly. Gwendolen wriggled out from underneath him and wiped her pussey with the corner of one of the discarded old costumes upon which they had been lying. "Time for another quick one?" she asked and before he could answer she leaned forwards on her hands and knees and presented the full moons of her soft rounded buttocks to Arthur's (and my own!) delighted gaze. His cock was still meaty looking but it swelled up again to a full erection after he slicked his hand up and down his wet shaft. Then when his prick was ready again for action he pulled open her rounded bottom-cheeks and, after wetting his knob with spittle, inserted the tip of his chopper inside the wrinkled brown rosette of her rear-dimple. She writhed with the pleasure and the shock afforded by this new sensation and Arthur had his work cut out to keep his cock in place.

'Her plump bum slapped nicely against the back of Arthur's thighs as he pounded away and reaching behind her she caressed his heavy ballsack as she rocked to and fro in time with Arthur's piston thrusts. My own cock had swollen up again but before I could even think of frigging myself for a second time, Arthur's torso suddenly went rigid and he spurted spasm after spasm of spunk into Gwendolen's arse-hole.

'But now came the disaster that nearly led to the abandonment of last night's performance of the play! For as Arthur emptied his balls he cried out not in ecstacy but in agony: "Ow! Ow! Ow! My back! My back!" as he fell forward on top of her, his prick still embedded in Gwendolen's back passage as they collapsed in an untidy heap. Poor Arthur was in obvious pain, his back muscles having seized up so badly that he was unable to move his body by even an inch. "Arthur, what's the matter? – please get off me!" cried Gwendolen in vain. They were joined together by Arthur's prick but she managed to wriggle free from this tender trap, leaving Arthur moaning in agony on the carpet of old costumes.

' "For God's sake get help, Gwen, I'm in terrible pain," moaned Arthur and hearing his plea I decided to make my presence known. I quickly walked back a few yards and then walked briskly towards the room, knocked on the door and threw it wide open. I feasted my eyes on Gwendolen's delicious naked charms for she was so agitated she made no attempt to cover her titties or her silky pubic muff of light brown curls.

' "Oh Michael, thank goodness you're here," she said with undisguised relief. I pretended to look shocked as I replied: "Good God, what's been going on here, Gwendolen? Did Arthur attack you?"

'Despite the desperate situation, she smiled briefly before replying: "Not in the way your question suggests; we were, er, um, doing some indoor exercise when suddenly Arthur keeled over and now he can't move!"

' "You'd better change, Gwendolen, your next scene opens in just over ten minutes' time," I said crisply, picking up Arthur's tights from the floor. "I'll go next door to Arthur's room and slip these on, pronto. Luckily we're near enough of the same build so I'll be able to change into his shirt and doublet as well. I'll take your boots as well, Arthur, if you don't mind. You know the first rule of all thespians – no matter what, the show must go on."

'Gwendolen clapped her hands together and looked admiringly at me. "Oh, Michael, I didn't realise what a masterful chap you are – but do you know Arthur's part?"

' "I've heard you rehearse often enough and we studied the play at school, but if I lose my place, young Sheena Walshaw is an excellent prompter and she'll help me out. Luckily the action takes place when the set won't be lit too brightly so hopefully the substitution won't be too glaring even for those people in the front stalls."

'I promised Arthur that I would send someone to help him as soon as possible and then went next door and changed into his costume. I grabbed Gwendolen's hand and pulled her along the corridor and upstairs to the side of the stage, where Sidney Smyth glared at her and whispered: "I was just about ready to send out a search party." Then when he saw me dressed as Vincentio his eyes bulged but he only had time to gurgle an imprecation before Gwendolen and I sailed onto the stage. The Gods were with me

144

and I managed to get through my lines without once having to take recourse of a prompt. In the wings, the rest of the cast gathered to find out what was happening, and as Gwendolen and I finished our scene to a storm of applause we were almost mobbed when the curtain came down at the end of the Act. I hastily explained what had befallen the stricken Arthur, tactfully omitting the prurient details of his unfortunate accident. Sidney went in front of the curtains and asked if there were a doctor in the house and fortunately Dr Fulham of the John Radcliffe Infirmary was in the audience and he kindly offered his services to us. During the interval, we managed to get Arthur up on his feet but I continued to play the role for the rest of the evening and Sidney made a further announcement to the audience explaining that the actor playing Vincentio had been taken ill and that I would act as understudy for the remainder of the play.

'Gwendolen was very grateful. Not only had I saved the day as far as the play was concerned but also that I had not breathed a word about how Arthur came to strain his back so badly! By the time we went back to our dressing rooms, Arthur had been helped back to his college and Gwendolen turned to me and suggested that I brought my clothes into her room so that we could change together. When I returned with my clothes she said: "I do so admire the way you solved our problem, Michael. But do you know, all this stress has given me all kinds of aches and pains. Would you care to massage my back for me?"

' "Certainly I would," I replied, "although I had better tell you that I have never tried to massage anybody before."

' "Oh, I'm sure that a clever chap like you will have no difficulties," she replied and before my very eyes she slipped out of her costume and gave me full view again of her delectable naked body. She lay face downwards on the small sofa and I licked my lips when Gwendolen wriggled her luscious bum cheeks. I moved over and put my hand on her shoulder. "Start from the top and work down," she suggested and nothing loath, I gently rubbed the smooth, warm skin of her neck with my fingertips.

' "M'mmm, you have a wonderful touch, Mr Beattie," she purred in a soft voice, "are you sure you have never before given any girl a massage?" For reply, I began kissing her, starting at the nape of her neck and then my kisses followed my hands which were soon clutching her glowing, rounded buttocks. As I frantically tore at the buttons of my doublet I rained rapid kisses down her backbone and over her bum cheeks down the backs of her thighs which made her body quiver all over.

'When I had managed to shuck off my tights, she turned round to lie on her back and her beautiful body lay sprawled before me, her legs flung invitingly apart and the white globes of her breasts acting as magnets to my hands which roved freely across them to feel the elongated red nipples. I kissed her pretty ankles and began travelling ever upwards. Gwendolen trembled with lustful anticipation when my hot lips reached the curly hair of her cunney and she moaned with desire when I sucked the pouting love lips into my mouth. She grabbed my hair and pulled me even closer as my tongue inserted itself into the damp crevice of her cunt. My tongue soon found her stiffening clitty and she gasped: "Yes, Michael, finish me off as quickly as you can!" So I gave her clitty my full attention, nibbling the hard flesh as her body jerked from side to side as I tongued her cunney and played with her titties until she threw back her head and in a paroxysm of erotic fervour cried out: "I'm coming, Michael, I'm going to come! Push your tongue in further! That's the way!" With a huge shudder she gained her release, mewing happily as her love juices dribbled over my lips and I swallowed as much of her pungent nectar as the flow ran over my face.

'When she had recovered she sat up and took my bursting prick in her hands. I tried to move on top of her, but she gently pushed me back and rising to her knees she said: "No, Michael, I don't want to go further now. Apart from anything else, it would hardly be fair to Arthur if I let you fuck me. But I tell you what, I'll relieve your feelings in a way which I think you'll like!"

'She slid her hand up and down my straining shaft as she lasciviously ran her tongue round her upper lip before stooping her head and kissing my uncapped helmet which sent a current of delicious sweetness flowing throughout my body. She played with my prick for some moments, slipping the crown in and out of her mouth whilst her tongue glided slowly up and down my pulsing pecker. She bobbed her head up and down so that I could fuck her mouth in a most delightful manner. Indeed, she sucked me off so beautifully that all too soon I could feel the rush of sperm hurtling up from my balls and with a cry I pumped out a stream of hot spunk between her rich, red lips. Gwendolen enjoyed this and she sucked up and swallowed every drop of my vital essence, milking my cock until it wilted under the frenetic urgency that it had encountered.

'There was no time for further petting even if we had wanted to continue as the theatre staff wanted to close up for the night. We dressed ourselves and made our way out and joined up with the other players at The Cat and Pigeons for a nightcap – but as you can all appreciate, I didn't stay too long for I was exhausted both physically and mentally by all that had happened earlier!'

Now Michael Beattie had told his stirring story so clearly that Frank, Barry and myself had listened with such rapt attention that none of us had noticed that several other fellows had quietly ended their conversations and had gathered round to listen to him. So at the conclusion of his colourful narrative, we were startled by the sound of a number of chaps who suddenly burst into a spontaneous round of applause. Poor Michael was dreadfully embarrassed and appealed to all those who had listened in to his tale to swear that they would not repeat his yarn to anyone else. Everyone readily agreed that to spread the story would be a caddish act – 'though in return I think Mike Beattie must tell us all the details when he finally fucks Gwendolen!' called out a fruity voice from behind me.

Michael raised his hands in surrender and said: 'We'll cross that bridge when we come to it – though I wouldn't be surprised if Gwendolen and I never actually go any further. Our snogging was spur-of-the-moment stuff and tonight when I'm playing Vincentio, as although Arthur's making a swift recovery he won't be able to resume his role until Friday's performance, I don't expect Gwendolen and I will do anything more than kiss each other on the stage.'

Frank called over the waiter and asked whether anyone would care to help him finish a second bottle of port. 'Not for me, thank you. I've really enjoyed listening to Michael's saga, but I must retire to my room as I've an essay to finish for tomorrow,' I said, rising to my feet.

'Oh come on, my friend, all work and no play makes Jack a dull boy, you know,' protested Barry. 'I was looking forward to a few rubbers of bridge this evening.'

'Get thee behind me, Satan,' I warned him with a smile. 'You know how much I enjoy a game of bridge, but please don't tempt me any further. I've a hellish day tomorrow though I'm quite looking forward to Professor Webb's party in the evening.'

'Have you also been invited to old Beaver's get-together?' drawled Frank. 'He asked me to come too but I didn't want to mention it before in case you hadn't been favoured with an offer to attend, what does he call it, his *conversazione*. It could be fun and I've been told that he owns the best cellar in the whole University.'

'Jolly good, Frank, I'm sure we'll have a fine time. Knock on my door at eight o'clock tomorrow night and we'll go to the bunfight together.' And before anything else could draw my attention, I waved a goodbye to my friends and made my way up to my room, resolving to burn the midnight oil until I had finished my essay.

CHAPTER THREE

A Test Of Endurance

IT WAS NEARLY TWO O'CLOCK IN the morning when with a sigh of relief I put down my pen and shuffled together the papers upon which I had written my essay which was about the tiresome political situation in Ireland. As I yawned and stretched my arms I thought to myself that this might not be the most elegant essay I had ever composed but though on the short side it was competent enough and would have to suffice. Indeed, I had been sorely tempted simply to write that there were no solutions to the Irish problem except build a border fence like the Great Wall of China between Ulster and the rest of the country though it would be hard to decide on which side lay the barbarians, but aphorisms of this kind would not please my tutor, Professor Cuthbert Cumberland, who was a man of acerbic wit and well-known to be merciless to students who sent in below standard work for his perusal.

He was also somewhat of a snob, a characteristic I abhor, although I still smile at the story about his involvement in a planned visit to the

University by the Crown Prince of Japan. An official from the Japanese Embassy visited Professor Cumberland to make the necessary arrangements and the Professor, who was a stickler for protocol, asked how the young man should be addressed. 'At home we refer to him as the Son of God,' said the diplomat, to which Professor Cumberland is supposed to have rejoined: 'That will present no problem. We are used to entertaining the sons of distinguished men at Oxford.' He had a perverse sense of humour too as shown by this probably apocryphal anecdote. It is said that a colleague rushed up to him one morning with the news that a member of the philosophy department had committed suicide. Professor Cumberland is said to have raised his hand and said: 'Please, don't tell me who. Allow me to guess!'

But I would just have to hope that my essay pleased the Professor for I was so sleepy that I could not have written another sentence. I fell asleep as soon as my head touched the pillow and would have missed breakfast and perhaps my first lecture if Nancy had not have woken me up in time. It was not part of her duties to rouse undergraduates from their slumber but the jolly girl wanted to apologise for slipping under the table and sucking me off during dinner the previous night. She had knocked on my door but when I had failed to reply she quietly entered as she had correctly guessed that I was still in bed.

I must say that I preferred Nancy's way of waking me up to that of any alarm clock! I felt my shoulder being shaken and as I came to my senses

I felt soft fingers snake their way around my stiff cock (since the age of thirteen I have always woken up with a boner) and I heard Nancy whisper: 'Wake up, Master Rupert, it's getting on for eight o'clock.' My head cleared quickly as her words seeped through and I slowly came to my senses, though for a few seconds I was puzzled by the fact that my tool was throbbing with pleasure even though I was not frigging myself. Then I quickly realised that Nancy was playing with my prick, rubbing her hand up and down the hot shaft, capping and uncapping my helmet as she said: 'Would you like me to finish you off, Master Rupert, or shall I run you a bath instead?'

'Time enough for both I think, Nancy, if you don't mind,' I said, now fully aware of what was going on. She grinned and increased the pace of motion, her hand flashing up and down my swollen shaft as I lay back and enjoyed the very pleasant sensation of being woken up by what is vulgarly known as 'a hand job'. Nancy's sensual rubbing soon brought the inevitable result and I spunked copiously, the sticky froth shooting out from my knob all over her hand and over my curly pubic hair.

This sight so excited her that she whispered: 'Oh dear, now we can't let all that luscious spunk go to waste,' and she bent down and sucked up as much of my emission as possible, licking my cock clean until my prick began to lose some of its stiffness. 'I do love sucking your cock, your sperm has just the salty tang that I like to swallow. Just the thought of taking your pole in my mouth makes me ever so randy,' she added, massaging

153

'I'd love to fuck you, Nancy, but it will have to be at another time as I'm already late for breakfast. Please run my bath now whilst I shave, there's a good girl,' I said, heaving myself out of bed.

She sighed and said: 'Well, how about this evening before dinner?'

I shook my head and said regretfully: 'Nancy, this must sound awfully conceited, but I'm afraid that I don't have the time. I'm only going to have half an hour or so to change before dinner and then I'm going to a reception at Professor Webb's house. Believe me, it's not that I don't want to fuck you but I'm not really free till after dinner tomorrow evening at the earliest and then only briefly because I'm going out again to an art class.'

'I can't meet you till Friday then because I'm going out myself tomorrow night,' she complained crossly. 'My friend Rosa and I have been given tickets to see *The Taming Of The Shrew* at the New Theatre.'

'Really? I do hope you enjoy it – who was the kind gentleman who provided your tickets?'

This question put her back into a good humour for she giggled and replied: 'Mike Beattie, of course. Why do you think I gobbled his cock under the table last night? Actually, I came in this morning to apologise if what I did during dinner upset you.'

'No, of course it didn't,' I hastened to assure her, 'although I must say I was very worried in case you were discovered.'

'It wouldn't have mattered too much, I would have just said that I was cleaning up some spilt

154

food,' she said coolly, 'and I'm sure that none of you would have given me away! I had only planned to suck off Michael but I'm particularly fond of your prick, Rupert, and I couldn't resist it.'

'Thank you, Nancy, I'm always very pleased to hear a girl say nice things about my prick because at school we were all a little jealous of Frank Folkestone's gigantic tool.'

Her remark at hearing this confession well illustrates why, as I have just written when recounting the anecdote about Professor Cumberland's snobbery, I detest this particular vice. More often that not, I was to discover that several college servants like Nancy possessed far more common sense than many of the fellows of the college including those who sat at the High Table. She laughed openly at this confession and exclaimed: 'For heaven's sake, don't disappoint me now, Master Rupert. Surely you're not one of those silly boys who measure themselves against what they see in the changing rooms and worry that their own pricks seem smaller than those dangling around them.'

I coloured slightly at her well chosen words which you may well recall, dear reader, gave further credence to Chrissie Nayland-Hunt's rebuke to Gillian Headleigh when the latter made an appreciative remark about the size of Salman Marrari's member.

Nancy continued: 'My last boyfriend, Billy Bucknall, who still works down the road in Blackwell's bookshop, had such a tremendous tadger that at school his form-mates used to whistle and cheer whenever they saw him take a shower. And of course he enjoyed basking in their approval and admiration, but this proud self-confidence soon vanished when he first had the opportunity to spoon seriously with the maid-of-all-work back in his parents' house.

'At first all was well and she allowed him to caress her breasts through her blouse and she rubbed her hand against the huge bulge in his lap – but when she unbuttoned his trousers and took out his prick she was so startled that she began to giggle. Now you can imagine what effect this had on a shy boy who had never even gone further than a furtive kiss before. His cock shrivelled down in double quick time and he couldn't coax it back up again for love or money. Still, I helped him to forget about his problem by explaining to him that a girl's cunney expands or contracts to take in whatever size cock is being placed inside it.'

'You must have had great fun giving Mr Bucknall a practical lesson,' I said drily.

'Yes, I taught Billy all he knows about fucking,' said Nancy with justifiable pride in her voice. 'We went out together for almost a year but neither of us want to settle down yet so we have agreed to go our separate ways for now, although you never know how things might turn out, do you?'

I gave Nancy a kiss as I stripped off and as I marched into the bathroom I called out: 'Nancy, thank you once again for waking me up this morning. Look, there's half a crown [*a coin worth 12½p which disappeared when Britain changed to decimal currency in 1971 – Editor*] on my bedside table. Please take it and buy yourself and Rosa a nice box of chocolates for the theatre tomorrow night.'

'That's not necessary, Master Rupert, really it isn't,' she protested as she followed me inside the bathroom and turned on the bath-taps while I rummaged around in the cupboard for my razor and shaving cream.

'I know it's not *necessary* but I'd like to show my gratitude to you, so please accept my gift as a sincere token of appreciation not as a fee for a service,' I said grandly and this pompous little speech made us both smile. Anyhow, Nancy finally accepted my little present and I just managed to get downstairs before the kitchen closed. After breakfast I left my essay in Professor Cumberland's pigeon-hole and spent the rest of the day hard at work. Nevertheless, I made sure to post two notes, one to the gorgeous Chrissie telling her that I would attend her art class the next night when she could give me further details about when and where we would meet my old pal Salman Marrari, and the other to the equally lovely Beth Randall, apologising for not having contacted her before but that I hoped she would be free to see me one day next week.

My crowded social calendar would certainly keep me busy, I thought, as I changed for dinner and Professor Webb's evening party. Still, we work to live, not live to work as our wealthy village squire and family friend Mr Buckingham was fond of saying when he called round in the morning to pick up my father for a day's fishing. Mind, my mother, who holds radical views upon what she calls the shockingly unfair distribution of wealth in our society, once asked the squire with some irritability how he would know this to be true as he had never done a day's work in his life!

'It's becoming quite difficult to fit everything in – as the maidservant said to the chauffeur!' I said to Frank Folkestone as we met as arranged after dinner.

'Don't complain,' advised Frank as we walked briskly out of the college gates. 'Despite the many opportunities to enjoy oneself here, there are very many first year students who are still lonely and homesick.'

'Very true, I have no right at all to grumble,' I sighed. 'And you seem to be getting on nicely, Frank. I can't believe that you really miss our life at St Lionel's.'

'Good God, I should say not, although I must admit that occasionally I do miss the friendship you and I shared with Prince Salman. We had some great times together, didn't we?'

This reminded me to tell Frank the good news about Salman coming to Oxford for the weekend. 'I'm sure you could join us for dinner tomorrow night,' I said but Frank shook his head.

'Damn, I've already arranged to dine with the Matthew Arnold Society, but try and bring him over for coffee on Saturday morning,' he said, a sensible suggestion with which I was happy to comply, though I speculated that Salman had planned to spend the morning in bed with the delectable Chrissie!

Professor Simon Webb's party turned out to be a fine affair – frankly, I had expected to mix in a small, exclusive gathering but there must have been at least fifty young people present. Frank and I were delighted to see that like Doctor Blayers, the good Professor believed in letting young people of both sexes engage in social intercourse and as I scanned the room looking to see if I knew any of the other guests besides Frank, I wondered whether Gillian Headleigh might be present.

'Are you looking for someone?' said a sweet feminine voice and I turned round and saw a truly ravishing girl standing beside me. She was a most beautiful creature, rather above medium height with shining bright brown hair, a fresh complexion and a pretty face which was set off by a merry smile that played upon her rich, red lips. Furthermore, this exquisite young lady was wearing a low cut crimson dress which revealed a goodly amount of her firmly-rounded breasts.

'Yes, I was looking to see whether Gillian Headleigh or her chum Chrissie Nayland-Hunt were here. Would you happen to know these girls by any chance?'

She looked at me closely and then with a lilting laugh in her voice she said with a fine theatrical flourish. 'I am acquainted with both of them and your question leads me to believe that your name is Rupert Mountjoy from Balliol College. Am I right or wrong, my dear sir?'

With a chuckle I raised my hands in surrender. 'The prisoner pleads guilty as charged. But we have not been introduced, so I can't imagine how on earth you come to know my name.'

'Elementary, my dear Watson,' she replied,

wagging a finger at me. 'Indeed so elementary that we hardly need employ the services of Sherlock Holmes or Sexton Blake. I am sharing lodgings with Gillian in Pusey Street whilst we are in Oxford and she has told me all about you, you naughty fellow.'

'Goodness me, I hope you don't believe everything that you are told.'

'It depends upon who is doing the telling and as you would-be lawyers might say, *cui bono? [who benefits? – Editor]*. As far as Gillian is concerned, I am sure that I can believe every word she has said about you, especially about your abilities to please members of the female sex.'

I blushed at the thought of what Gillian had told this gorgeous girl about our escapades. 'Of course you can, I didn't mean to even hint that Gillian would ever deliberately utter an untruth.'

'Of course you didn't,' she agreed. 'But alas, neither she nor Chrissie are here to defend themselves even if you did. They've gone to see the Dramatic Society's production of *The Taming Of The Shrew* at the New Theatre this evening.'

Well, dear reader, this led me on to mention my friend Michael Beattie's involvement in the play, though naturally I did not breathe a word about the truth of just how he came to take over the part except to say that Arthur Cuthbertson had suddenly taken ill during a performance and that at very short notice, Michael had bravely stepped into the breach.

'Anyhow, whilst I am sorry that Gillian and Chrissie aren't here, I'm delighted that their absence has brought us together, Miss, ah, now you have the advantage of me as you know my name but I don't know yours!'

'I'm Marianne Dawson and I'm pleased to meet you, Rupert, and please don't worry, Gillian said only the nicest things about you!'

This chance meeting was indeed fortuitous for me. Marianne and I chatted animatedly especially when I discovered that we shared an interest in photography. I told her of how Frederick Nolan, the American cinematographer, had come to my family's home [see An Edwardian Dandy 1: Youthful Scandals *for a full account of Rupert's involvement in making one of the earliest 'blue' films made in Britain – Editor*] and I was saying how popular moving pictures had become with the general public, when Professor Webb himself joined in the conversation.

'Moving pictures, young Mountjoy?' he snorted. 'Can't abide them, to be frank with you – all that jerky flickering gives me a headache after a time but I suppose they'll form an interesting library of material for future historians to complement the newspapers and official records. I grant you that now people are flocking to see cinematograph shows but these only have novelty value and won't pose any threat against the music halls and the theatre.'

Marianne took issue immediately with this view. 'I can't agree with you, sir. The film offers a new entertainment to an international audience. A film-maker such as Frederick Nolan makes his film and can have copies shown all over the world. All Frenchmen, Spaniards, Italians or what have you need do is to insert title slides in their

161

own language where needed. I grant you that the actors cannot be heard but against this, the action is more realistic, being able to switch at will from inside to outdoors and from the past to the present and if necessary even to the future. Of course, whilst the film remains without the power of speech, the theatre remains unchallenged but I would wager that sooner rather than later, some clever inventor will marry sound and colour to film and there will be machines available that we can buy so that we can view these films in the comfort of our own homes.'

'Oh, I think you are now entering the realms of fantasy, my dear,' said the Professor doubtfully although I strongly backed up Marianne's prophecy. [*In the fullness of time, an ironic coincidence would see Rupert in New York on the evening of October 6th, 1927, squiring a pretty actress to the premiere of 'The Jazz Singer', the very first film in which the cast were heard to talk – Editor*]

'Well, one matter upon which we can surely all agree is that the moving picture will never replace the art of painting, although like the majority of my friends, I was most disappointed at this summer's Royal Academy Exhibition,' I declared roundly.

Professor Webb beamed and said: 'I am pleased to hear you say so, young Mountjoy. I looked in vain for evidence of new genius coming to the fore but was castigated for my criticism by my young brother who sits on the Hanging Committee. He had the cheek to call me an old fogey! Well, he could hardly level the same charge at you and your chums!'

'I was not able to see this year's Exhibition as I spent the summer with my family in America,' confessed Marianne, 'but I don't think we should judge the newer artists too hastily. The language of art varies – what may have been expressive yesterday may be regarded as merely commonplace today. But from what I've seen at previous exhibitions, I would say that the danger comes in that once an artist is admitted into the Academy, he often becomes too contented with himself to care to do anything that he had not done before.'

'There we are most certainly in agreement,' said the Professor, running a hand through his bushy red beard. 'I've been collecting landscapes by Stanley Brendah *[a British landscape artist whose Hertfordshire scenes became extremely popular and fetched high prices around the turn of the century – Editor]* for the last ten years and I would have to agree with you that since he was given the *imprimateur* of an Academician, his work has suffered. The bold, dashing style seems to have become muted, as if he were afraid of experimentation in case his admirers might turn away, just as I must turn away from this interesting debate, dear Miss Marianne, for I must circulate amongst my guests and make some introductions where necessary. Many young people are terribly shy and stand around all by themselves, lonely in the thronging crowd, and I consider it my bounden duty as host to help them break into a friendly circle.'

As Professor Webb plunged through the crowd, I said to Marianne: 'What a decent old stick! It's very thoughtful of him to make sure that his more reticent guests enjoy themselves. Mind, I never knew he was a connoisseur of landscape pictures.'

'Ah, there's probably quite a lot you don't know about our host,' said Marianne brightly. 'He specialises in other artistic fields too.'

'Really? In poetry perhaps, or in sculpture?'

'Neither, Rupert, and I doubt if you would ever guess the answer. You see, the Professor's chosen speciality is in sucking pussey.'

I looked at her blankly for I could hardly believe my ears. 'Yes, it's true, I do assure you,' she said, trying hard to suppress a giggle. 'How do you think he came to have a nickname such as "Beaver"?'

'Well, blow me down, I would never have suspected it,' I said, taking a large gulp from my glass of the excellent fruit punch. 'My, this also has quite a bite to it.'

We looked at each other and spontaneously collapsed into roars of laughter at this unintentional witticism. Frank strolled over to see what all the fun was about but we could hardly repeat the story and he retired muttering that we must have been pouring the punch down our throats too quickly for our own good. 'I say, Marianne, you're not having me on about "Beaver" Webb, are you?' I asked when we finally recovered our composure.

'No, of course not, Rupert,' she replied indignantly. 'Why, I myself had the pleasure of being brought off by his brilliant oral skills earlier this evening. I came here an hour before the party was due to begin because I had heard of his reputation as a cunnilinguist from my cousin Lucinda, who studied under Simon Webb last year. I was attracted to the idea of having my pussey pleasured in this fashion by an expert for the art is alas not practised as widely in this country as it is on the Continent and in America.

'As I had arrived so early, I was shown into a small sitting-room to wait until the Professor had finished dressing though it was not long before he came bursting in, saying that he was sorry not to have received me before but he had not expected such an early arrival. He opened a bottle of fizz whilst I told him that I knew I was early but that I shared his interest in art and wondered if he would be interested in an early Stanley Brendah picture I had uncovered, as my cousin Lucinda had told me of his interest in this artist. It was an unusual painting for it was a nude study and I had always thought of Brendah as a landscape specialist. Simon's face lit up and he explained: "Ah, well you see, Stanley was quite a ladies' man in his early days and every time, how shall I say, he sowed some wild oats, he made figure studies of the girls concerned."

' "How fascinating! So his lovers have been immortalised on canvas! I would have loved to have been one of his models but I don't think I have quite the figure for it."

' "Stuff and nonsense, my dear Miss Dawson, I am sure that any artist worth his salt would be honoured to have you pose for him," he replied. I looked at him with a wide-eyed innocence and said: "Do you really think so, Professor?"

' "Oh come now, let's not be so formal, we're

not in the lecture hall now. My name is Simon," he said. "Very well, Simon, thank you, but then you must call me Marianne," I replied as I hitched my skirts up to my knees. I stretched out my legs and enquired: "Tell me truthfully, Simon, don't you think my calves are a little too plump for someone like Stanley Brendah to paint me?"

' "No, no, not at all, they are quite beautiful in my judgement," he said, swallowing hard as I crossed and uncrossed my legs. Then I stood up and moved forwards towards him. When I reached his chair I deliberately leaned forward so that my bosom almost spilled out of this low-cut dress. Now false modesty is as foolish and vulgar as overweening pride, so I have no hesitation in telling you that like all men, Simon Webb was overwhelmed by the nearness of my soft, rounded breasts. He gulped again as I said seductively: "What I would really appreciate is for you to give me your opinion on perhaps my best attributes." He gaped in silence, his mouth hanging open in amazement as I fiddled with the hook behind my back to loosen the top of my gown and he stood up and helped me unbutton my dress so I was able to step out of it without creasing the material too badly. With a graceful movement I pulled off my chemise so that my bare breasts were exposed to his excited gaze and then I took his trembling hands and pressed them to my titties which made the nipples pop up like two little bullets.

'It was time for me to display the *pièce de resistance* so with a deliberately accentuated wriggle I pulled down my frilly lace knickers. As I stepped out of them I bent down and picked them up from the floor. I held my knickers in my hand as I stroked my sides sensuously before placing my knickers on the silky mound of hair between my legs and rubbing them against it. Now the merest touch of my fingers against my pussey is always enough to get me going, so throwing all modesty aside I tossed them to Simon as I teasingly purred: "Sniff them and tell me if you like the aroma of my pussey. Then if you wish to sample what you see on display, I would very much like you to suck my pussey. Otherwise I will assume that you want me to wrap the goods up again and place them back on the shelf!"

'He did not reply but wordlessly he rose and took me in his arms. Then he planted his mouth on mine and we exchanged a lingering kiss before I felt myself being gently laid back on the floor. Simon pulled down a cushion from a chair to act as a pillow for me as I lay back and relaxed, thrilling to the movement of his lips sliding down my body. He kissed each raised tittie in turn as his hands prised open my unresisting thighs. Then he buried his face between my legs and licked the dampness round my pussey lips as I lifted my bottom so that he could clasp my buttocks and pull them forward to him. My cunney opened out like a flower as he slipped his tongue through the pouting pink pussey lips and lapped with long, thrusting strokes between the inner grooves of my cunt, which by now was beginning to gush out love juice.

'Simon certainly deserved first class honours for his ability to bring a girl off with his mouth. To add to my pleasure he slipped two fingers into my slit which made me thrash around wildly until the electric sensations subsided. But what took me up to the highest realms of ecstatic pleasure was how he attacked my clitty, driving his tongue into the ring of my love channel and then as the tiny bean broke from its pod he gripped it in his strong fingers and tugged at it quite vigorously, which made me spend profusely as I writhed my hips dementedly. Then he lowered his mouth again and slurped noisily on my drenched pussey, his tongue driving fast round the juicy crack from which dribbled a flow of tangy love juice which he swallowed with evident relish.

'I would have liked nothing better to have repaid the compliment by sucking his prick but the first of the other guests would soon be arriving and I needed time to put my clothes back on. Simon also understood why I would not let him fuck me with his sizeable prick which he had let free from the confines of his trousers. I am sure you will agree, Rupert, that it would have been far too forward to let oneself be fucked after so brief an introduction.'

'Oh absolutely so,' I said gravely, nodding my head in agreement. 'I never fuck with any girl I have known for less than thirty minutes.'

Marianne's delicious dimples showed as she smiled broadly at my ironic comment and said: 'A very wise maxim to follow – and one should be most careful when recounting the pleasures of one's fucking, though I know I can trust you to keep the tale I have just told you under your hat. For as Molière rather cynically wrote: *le scandale du monde est ce qui fait l'offense, et ce n'est pas pêcher que pêcher en silence'* [*It is a public scandal that gives offence and it is no sin to sin in secret – Editor*].

'So poor Professor Webb must be feeling rather frustrated unless he has sought relief from the five-fingered widow,' I commented.

'Perhaps, though I think it more likely that he asked one of the girls in that group over by the window to toss him off.'

'That would be rather dangerous, wouldn't it?'

'Not really, for I am certain that he has probably fucked at least three of them. Amanda Wellsend, the tall blonde girl, told me only this evening that she rode a splendid St George on Simon's cock the other afternoon.'

Marianne looked down and lightly touched the bulge in my lap with her hand. 'I think that you might be more frustrated than Professor Webb,' she murmured. 'Do erotic anecdotes make you feel randy too? I must say that after telling you that lewd story, I'm also feeling pretty horny myself.'

My blood *was* on fire and I muttered: 'What a pity there are no private rooms to which we could repair.'

'But there are, my dear – wait here for just a moment and I'll arrange everything for us,' she replied, a lascivious smile forming across her lips as her hand dived down to give my swollen cock a friendly squeeze.

Marianne then made her way through the chattering crowd to where Professor Webb was holding court with his *amorata* Amanda Wellsend and her friends. I saw her whisper something in his ear after which he passed something small from his waistcoat pocket to her which she clutched in her fist. When she returned to me she opened her hand to reveal a key. 'For one of the bedrooms upstairs?' I hazarded.

She gave a wolfish grin and said: 'Who's a clever boy, then?' and she took my hand and pulled me towards the staircase. I was hardly unwilling to accompany her but as we climbed the stairs I glanced back to see how Frank was fairing – and I was pleased to see that he had now joined Professor Webb's little group and was deep in discussion with a striking red-haired girl who was laughing at some witty remark Frank had just made if the rather smug expression on his face was a true guide to what was happening down there.

When we reached the landing Marianne pulled me across into the passage leading to the bedrooms and unlocked the door to our left. We went in and she closed the door behind us as I switched on the electric light. The room was richly furnished and I was delighted to see there was a large double bed for us – fucking on a narrow single mattress can be fine but I am sure you will agree, dear reader, that *un lit matrimonial* offers more room for both partners. Be that as it may, Marianne and I wasted no time in tearing off our clothes and in under a minute we were rolling around quite naked on the Professor's huge bed, our mouths glued together in a passionate kiss, our tongues lashing away inside the other's mouth, hugging and clutching each other in a frenzy of loving voluptuousness.

Finally, I was forced to break away from our embrace to draw breath – and raising myself on my elbow I looked down upon the soft, quivering body of this exquisite girl. She had unpinned her hair and her gorgeous face was now set off by soft waves of chestnut hair which cascaded down over her shoulders. Her firm, jutting breasts stood out proudly whilst her well-rounded shoulders tapered down into a surprisingly small waist. Yet her thighs were full and beautifully proportioned whilst between her long legs lay a furry fleece of brown hair which formed a delicious veil over her pouting pink cunney lips.

Marianne whispered: 'Let's start with a *soixante-neuf*. Why don't you lick my cunt whilst I suck your cock?' I have always maintained that this is the most ingenious yet easiest erotic position after the simple man-on-top-woman-underneath-on-her-back 'missionary' position, so called because our more bigoted evangelicals have always taught that this is the only permissible way to engage in intercourse.

I have always delighted in the magic of *soixante-neuf* and Marianne and I assumed the position which led to me repositioning myself so that my legs were up against the bedstead with my cock by Marianne's mouth whilst my own lips were just inches away from the succulent goal of her sweet pussey. I inhaled and savoured the piquant fragrance before burying my face between her legs in this aromatic nest of love. I kissed her creamy crack and my tongue began whipping back and forth, taking on a life of its own when I slipped the tip of my tongue between her cunney lips which opened in salute as it bored deep inside her juicy wet cunt. I felt for her clitty and ran my tongue up and down the sides, teasing it into a full erection as taking it now between my lips I tweaked its plump unsheathed base with the tip of my tongue, which sent tremors of lustful passion hurtling through her.

Meanwhile Marianne closed her lips around the bulbous uncapped knob of my raging stiffstander and it was my turn to shudder as her tongue flicked over my helmet, down the shaft and over my balls before reversing the route back to the mushroom dome. Her moist mouth worked its way over every inch of my rock-hard cock, her hand grasping the base as she pumped her head up and down, keeping her lips taut, kissing and sucking my pulsating prick as she ground her now sopping cunt against my face – our tempos matching in increasing speed, faster and faster as our twitches grew into tremors, the tremors into convulsions as first Marianne climaxed, moaning her joy as she flooded my mouth with her liquid spendings. Soft and yielding, the delicate cunney flesh was slippery against my tongue and I was engulfed in her spasms which sent waves of love juice coursing their way through her love channel and into my mouth and over my face.

Now I felt the first unmistakable rise of spunk rising up from my balls as Marianne continued to suck my throbbing tool, somehow managing to take almost all my shaft deep down into her throat. Her tongue slid juicily up and down until, with a low growl I cried out: 'Ahhh, here it comes!' and I shot an explosive stream of sticky white froth into her mouth which she gulped down as best she could though my emission was so strong that some of my spunk dribbled down her chin. I sat up and she leaned forward, tasting ourselves as we exchanged a long, lingering kiss.

Much like artichokes and olives, cunnilingus is an acquired taste but I would urge all young men who wish to pleasure their partners to try it. After all, is there a chap to be found anywhere in this world, regardless whether he prefers blondes, brunettes, or redheads in bed or indeed even if he is of the homosexualist persuasion, who does *not* love having his cock sucked? And if your bed-mate pleasures you, should you not play the game and return the compliment? Pussey-eating is an art in its infancy in this country which is, I am convinced, one of the reasons why English girls seem to fall so readily into the beds of the Latin races who practice cunnilingus almost as a matter of course.

Certainly, as far as Marianne was concerned, having her pussey pleasured by my mouth made her terribly randy. 'Rupert,' she said throatily, her voice crackling with desire, 'I want you to fuck me now, so slide your lovely cock in my cunt straightaway, if you please.'

Well, though putting myself in danger of sounding like an alehouse braggart, I should record here that my ability to keep a stiff prick at the ready has often been a source of joy and sometimes delighted surprise to my bed-mates, and at the age of eighteen, when the incident I am now describing took place, my prowess was at its peak and I could spend six or seven times a night without over-exerting myself in any great fashion.

So to return to the tale, despite spurting copiously into Marianne's mouth, my cock retained much of its tumescence and the soft touch of Marianne's fingers soon had my shaft standing stiffly to attention. She lay back on the bed, and I raised myself on top of her superb body and looked down upon the delicious curves of her breasts with their elongated erect nipples pointing outwards. My eyes then travelled downwards to her milky white thighs, which were as perfectly proportioned as any Grecian statue and spread wide to reveal every exquisite fold of her juicy cunt.

Slowly I eased myself down upon her, my cock sliding between her slicked cunney lips into the clinging moistness of her love channel, driving deeper and deeper until my prick was fully embedded inside her and our pubic hairs mashed together. Instantly, our bodies began to thrash back and forth in a fit of lustful passion. Clinging madly to each other, Marianne clamped her legs around my waist, squealing with delight as I pumped away and her hips writhed and twisted in time with my thrusts to maximise her pleasure. What a marvellous fuck this was! Her cunney had been so well-oiled by her previous spend that I was able to slide my cock in up to the hilt and her pussey absorbed every inch of my shaft, rippling over my length as her body exploded into a series of tiny spends. She tossed her head from side to side, biting her lower lip for she was worried that letting out her emotions in an ardent scream might be heard above the din of the partying guests downstairs. But when my own orgasm arrived and I flooded her cunney with a vibrant stream of hot, frothy spunk, she could not contain herself and whilst spout after spout of sticky sperm poured from my cock deep inside her velvety cavern, she let out an uninhibited howl of pure ecstacy as she shuddered to a magnificent climax.

Now despite my previous remark about being able to fuck all night at the peak of my youthful vigour, I was now gasping for breath, almost insensible from my efforts and I flopped down beside Marianne and my cock languished limply over my thigh. 'Oh my, I hope you have not over-exerted yourself,' said Marianne anxiously as she placed her head on my chest and listened with concern to the thumping beats of my heart. I ran my fingers through her hair and smiled contently, at peace with the world.

'Just give me some time to recover, my love, and I'll be as fit as a fiddle,' I said, closing my eyes for a well-deserved little nap, and so Marianne obediently snuggled down and moulded her soft curves into my body as we held each other tight for our short journey to the Land of Nod. She woke first and roused me by kissing me all over my body. By the time her head burrowed down to reach my burgeoning prick I was already awake and I grunted my appreciation as she washed my uncapped knob all over with her tongue. She pulled her head back and flipped herself round to lie on her belly, pulling a pillow underneath her so the rounded globes of her backside were pushed out cheekily as with a sensuous little wriggle she signalled her readiness to be bottom-fucked.

I needed no further invitation and immediately heaved myself up to kneel behind her. Carefully I pulled apart those delectable bum cheeks and angled her legs a little further apart to afford a better view of her puckered little nether orifice. Then I gently eased my knob between her buttocks and pushed into the tight little rosette. My cock was still moist from our previous spendings and I encountered little difficulty for her sphincter muscle soon relaxed and I slid my tadger in and out of the tight sheath, plunging my prick to and fro as Marianne reached back and spread her cheeks even further to widen the rim for me, jerking her arse in time to my rhythm as I wrapped one arm around her breasts, frigging each of her titties in turn and with my other hand I diddled her sopping pussey, rubbing her clitty, which afforded her the greatest of delight, doubling her pleasure now being fucked from both in front and behind.

Her bottom responded to every shove as I jerked my hips to and fro and my balls fairly bounced against her smooth bum as I cornholed her to the very limit. The unique, almost indescribable tingling one experiences in the cockshaft towards the end of a fuck soon heralded the approaching arrival of my spend. I moved my stout shaft faster and faster as Marianne worked her bum with a will until she brought me off and I injected her rear with a lavish libation of gushing jism which warmed and lubricated her delicious bottom. When I had finished emptying my balls I withdrew my cock from her well-lathered back passage with an audible plop and sank back to rest after this lascivious episode for a well-earned rest. We had been at it for only just over an hour and already I had fucked her three times and from the gleam in Marianne's eyes, I suspected that the night was still young as far as she was concerned!

Sure enough, in a short time our bodies were locked together as we mashed our mouths against each other's lips. With a fluttering tongue, she explored the inside of my mouth whilst I ran my hands over her proud thrusting breasts, letting my fingers delve into the crevice between the two white rounded beauties.

'Am I naughty to love fucking so much?' she sighed thoughtfully. 'Would you be shocked if I confessed to you that I like nothing better than a thick prick sliding in and out of my pussey?'

'Of course not, so long as you take care to guard against unwanted consequences and choose your lovers with care,' I murmured, brushing away a stray lock of hair from her face.

'Well, naturally I wouldn't have let you spunk inside me without a johnny [a condom – Editor] if I had not already taken precautions,' she said indignantly. 'And I would be very upset if the thought ever crossed your mind that I let any Tom, Dick or Harry fuck me.'

'It never crossed my mind and I assure you that I did not mean to imply any such dreadful imputation,' I said hastily. 'Furthermore I don't think you are wrong to love fucking – I also can't think of a nicer way to spend my time and after all, if the parsons are right to condemn intercourse except for the purpose of procreation, why did our Creator make love-making so pleasurable if he did not want us to enjoy it?'

To my astonishment my rhetorical question was answered! 'I could not agree more with you. Apes have been observed to finish their sexual union in six seconds, the male using some seven or eight thrusts of the phallus to complete the act. Would the puritanically inclined wish us to behave in such fashion? Is this a benchmark to which we should aspire?' said a fruity male voice by the door.

I sat up in shock at this interruption but Marianne appeared to be very little disturbed by the stranger's entrance. 'Don't fuss, Rupert,' she said soothingly. 'It's only our host who I am sure has come up here only to make sure that we are having a jolly time.'

By Gad, she was absolutely right regarding the identity of the intruder for this uninvited visitor was indeed none other than our host, Professor Webb. He stood at the foot of the bed and flourished what must have been a spare key of the door before putting it back in his pocket. He beamed at us and said: 'You're not too tired to accommodate a fresh cock, are you, Marianne?'

'So long as it's rock-hard and ready to do its duty,' she answered. And before I could venture to give my opinion on the matter, our host was unbuckling his trousers and sitting down on the bed to bend down and take off his shoes and socks. 'I do owe Simon a good fuck, you remember. I had no time even to suck his cock before the party began after he had creamed my cunney so superbly with his mouth.'

'Be my guest, Professor,' I said rather sourly and moved across the bed as our uninvited guest climbed into bed with us. Although the bed was large, we only just had enough room to allow him in with us. For he was naturally broad shouldered and over the years had developed a corpulent figure which tended to sag somewhat without the power of clothing to pull him into shape. But there was nothing amiss with his massive love truncheon which stood out from a mass of grey-flecked ginger hair at the base of his belly. He climbed rather awkwardly on top of Marianne and I must say that I was concerned that her tight little crack might make it difficult to take in such a mighty weapon.

But perhaps because she had just absorbed my own sizeable prick, even a shaft the girth of the Professor's presented no problems for her and I watched in awe as the gigantic crown of the Professor's cock slid between Marianne's pouting cunney lips. He took a deep breath and then let out a deep growl of satisfaction as inch by inch his thick tool disappeared inside her warm, juicy pit.

'There, do you like my thick prick slipping into your juicy cunt, m'dear?' he asked roguishly.

'Yes, I love it. Push it all in, you randy cocksman!' she gasped, but teasingly he pulled back and she wailed with dismay as with a passionate jolt of his loins the randy pedagogue plunged it in again, which made her roll her hips and clasp her legs around his waist whilst his large hairy ballsack banged against her bum.

They fucked away in joyful unison, with Marianne clutching his ample buttocks to draw him even closer inside her and they heaved merrily away as he screwed his shaft in and around her luscious crack.

'Oh what a perfect pussey! How it sucks and clasps my cock! A-h-r-e, I'm coming, I'm coming, I can't hold back!' he groaned and she panted:

'It's all right, don't worry – I'm almost there too. Shoot your spunk, you thick-pricked fucker!'

These lewd words sent them both passing the point of no return and the lewd pair gloried in the joys of an unforced simultaneous spend as they writhed around in ecstacy with Marianne's pussey awash with the Professor's jism as well as the love juices flowing freely from her own cunney. Then, when they had completed the course, he moved off her, flopping over to lie down on her side that was furthest from me.

Watching this erotic exhibition had so excited my flaccid cock that it had swollen back up again in a fine state of erect stiffness. I rolled over back to Marianne and began to kiss and cuddle her. The insatiable girl relished the idea of a further fuck and responded by embracing me whilst I played with her titties. I guided my hand between her legs and parting her cunney lips with my fingers, began to massage her wet pussey which made her purr with pleasure. Shortly her bottom began to jerk up and down to the rhythm of my frigging and she opened her legs wider to receive me as I clambered on top of her. We were both leaning on our sides as with a squelchy swishy sound my cock slid into her sopping love channel. Marianne rotated her hips, working her soft, wet flesh against my hot, hard shaft as I matched her rhythm, letting my length slide in and out of her clinging dampness until our surging cries of fulfilment echoed round the room as her cunt milked my prick which was thrusting faster and faster out of her sated body.

'Aaah! Aaah! One last push!' she screamed out and she bucked and twisted under me as her spend sent thrilling waves of electric delight crashing through every fibre of her being. She arched her hips and with a huge final shudder, sank happily into the bliss that follows the draining of love's reservoir.

When we had all regained our strength, the three of us spent the rest of the night engaged in further fucking and sucking. I think my favourite position was fucking Marianne's cock-hungry cunney whilst she lustily sucked on the Professor's prick, though we tried several variations on this and similar themes until the first rays of daylight heralded the dawn.

After bidding the others farewell (for neither Marianne nor the Professor needed to rise at an early hour), I walked back to college with some difficulty, taking only small, bandy-legged steps as my over-indulgence had left me saddle-sore. God knows how long Marianne will need to recover from her all-night orgy, I thought as I hauled myself up the stairs to my room. There's just time for forty winks before breakfast, I decided whilst taking off my coat and dinner jacket, and without further ado I threw myself down upon my bed. But I was so completely worn out from the violent erotic excesses in which I had participated, that, this time being without the kind assistance of Nancy, I fell into a deep sleep from which I did not awake until shortly after eleven o'clock.

Still, both my mind and body felt refreshed when I finally awoke, and after undertaking what my fellow undergraduates rather vulgarly know as a triple S *[a shower, shit and shave – Editor]*, I was ready to face the day. Unfortunately, I had missed a seminar on the law of property, which meant that I had inadvertently broken the promise which those readers with good memories will recall I had made to my godfather about diligent attendance at lectures during my first year as a student. However, I did not feel too badly about this as the offence was not one committed deliberately and most fellows cut some work at some time or other without getting into any trouble. Mind, this did not hold good for one poor fellow who was summoned to the office of the famous Oxford don Dr Spooner, who when excited would often transpose the initial sounds of pairs of words, and was told by the angry don: 'You have hissed all my mystery lectures and are suspended from your studies. Leave college immediately by the next town drain.' *[W A Spooner (1844-1930) gave his name to such slip-ups of speech now known as Spoonerisms. One of his most notorious bloopers was standing up to toast Queen Victoria when she visited his college in 1889 and saying: 'Ladies and gentlemen, here's to the queer old dean.' – Editor]*.

To make up for taking the morning to recover from the night before, I resolved to spend the rest of the day in the library. But as I was about to leave my room I noticed that a letter had been placed under the door. I did not recognise the writing which I deduced to be in a feminine hand but decided to take the envelope with me and read the letter in the common-room over a cup of coffee before I shut myself up in the library.

Who could be writing to me? I opened the envelope and found to my disappointment that the scribe was Chrissie Nayland-Hunt and that she was the bearer of sad tidings . . .

For the record, I reproduce her letter and the missive which accompanied it:

Dear Rupert,

I am sorry to tell you that Salman Marrari has been forced to postpone his visit to Oxford this weekend. I enclose his letter which is self-explanatory. Do let me have it back as he writes so well that I become greatly excited just reading it.

Still, I hope we can still dine together on Friday night though I will quite understand if you prefer to cancel our arrangement.

Love,
Chrissie

Salman's letter read as follows:

Darling Chrissie,

It is with heartfelt apologies that I must write to say it will not be possible to come to Oxford on Friday. My uncle Pandit, who is one of the members of an important Indian governmental consultative council on native education, has arrived in Britain for a short visit and naturally he wishes to see me this coming weekend in London.

You will understand, I am sure, that this is an invitation which I cannot refuse. Perhaps you will let me know whether you will be free in two weeks' time and I can come over to see you and Rupert then. Perhaps you would ask Rupert to tell Frank Folkestone of my visit so we can have a reunion of our old gang from St Lionel's. I know you'll be back here in Cambridge by then but would you mind going back to Oxford as I would so like to see my old school chums again.

However, wherever we do meet is no great matter so long as we see each other very soon. Chrissie, it is you who I will miss most on Friday, for I had planned a weekend of l'amour which will now have to wait for at least a fortnight. Shall I tell you what I had in mind and what I still hope will happen when we finally do manage to see each other again?

Do you remember how we first made love this summer after watching the lawn-tennis championships at Wimbledon? We had just eaten strawberries and cream and were sitting in my carriage which had the blinds drawn when I leaned over and kissed you and then one thing led to another and the carriage rocked so violently that we startled the horses which began to neigh and chafe at the bit. Wasn't it lucky that they calmed down before old Johnstone the driver returned!

Ah, the memory makes my prick harden up as I recall that delightful afternoon! But enough of the past – let me look forward to the future and I'll tell you what I have in store once we are together. I shall place you naked on a cool white sheet on my bed and smear your quivering soft body all over with cream from a large bowl into which I will dip

184

my bursting cock and then, taking hold of my shaft and using it like a paintbrush, plaster your sumptuous breasts and the crisp dark curls of your pussey hair with cream from my cock. Then I'll take a big banana, peel it and roll it over your titties until it is covered in cream and then slide it between your moist pussey lips deep inside your cunney, leaving only a little piece sticking out. Then I'd place my head between your legs and eat the sticky fruit, drawing it out slowly piece by piece as I taste the delicious mixed aroma of banana and cream laced with cunney juice!

Here Chrissie scribbled a note in the margin: 'I'd love to have my bubbies smothered in cream, perhaps with a cherry on each nipple – so long as I had the right man to eat them and lick it all off, of course!'

Now you know, dear Chrissie, that we promised never to keep any secrets from each other. So I will not hold back from recounting what occurred last Thursday afternoon when I went into town to buy you an 'unbirthday' present which I had planned to bring with me to Oxford this weekend. My original idea was to buy you a book but whilst browsing through the shelves at Heffer's, I bumped into Johnny Crawford, a fellow member of the University Polo Club, and when I told him that I was searching for a present for my girlfriend, he suggested that I go down the road and purchase something suitable in Madame Antoinette's French lingerie shop in Green Street instead. I protested that I had never been inside such a shop before but he dismissed my fears, saying with a strange smile upon his face: 'There is no need to feel apprehensive.

From my own experience, Salman, I can tell you that Madame Antoinette's girls give a splendid personal service to all their clients, both ladies and gentlemen alike.'

Well, it was worth a look, I thought, so I thanked Johnny and made my way to Madame Antoinette's, a small establishment tucked away in an alley set between two large emporiums. I felt slightly embarrassed at going into such a shop but nobody had seen me go into the alley so I screwed up my courage and opened the lace-curtained door. At first there appeared to be no-one inside the place as well, but in a few moments a young sales girl came through from the back of the shop.

'Bonjour, monsieur, can I help you?' she asked. I looked at her with interest. She was a slim brunette with long, curly hair and despite having probably worked in the shop all day, her flawless skin still had a fresh, vibrant glow. She was dressed in a dark skirt and a white open necked blouse which exposed enough cleavage to make my prick stir in my trousers, especially when she leaned forward to pick up her tape measure which had fallen to the floor. 'Madame Antoinette?' I asked nervously and she showed a set of dazzling white teeth when she smiled and replied: 'Mais non, monsieur, my name is Cherie, Madame Antoinette's niece, and I am helping her run her shop whilst I am staying in Cambridge to gain more practice in speaking English. Tell me, are you also learning English here, monsieur, ah, I don't think you mentioned your name?'

'Salman, Prince Salman Marrari at your service, mademoiselle. And no, I am studying science at the

186

University, because English happens to be my mother tongue, the language in which I think and the one in which I can best express myself to other people. But I am fluent enough in Hindi and Gujarati, which occasionally we speak back home to our servants or when we don't want the British to understand us!'

She chuckled at this and I added that I wanted to buy something for my girlfriend who I was seeing soon for a weekend reunion. 'I would like something elegant yet revealing for she has a lovely figure, much like yours,' I said boldly and Cherie put her hand on my arm and said: 'Then in that case I will model one or two garments for you.' She looked up at the clock and said: 'Good, it is near enough closing time,' and she drew a bolt across the door and hung the closed sign on it. I sat down whilst she went back into the back office which doubled as a showroom. In just a few minutes she emerged wearing a negligee of such fine silk that it was almost transparent. She was wearing nothing underneath the negligee and I could make out the rounded globes of her bottom as she executed a little pirouette in front of me and the dark buttons of her nipples pushed out provocatively from their light covering.

Cherie must have seen my cock shoot up when she smoothed her fingers over her firm breasts, for then she rubbed her nipples against the palms of her hands and said softly: 'Does your girlfriend have sensitive titties, Salman?' Unable to speak, I simply nodded and she continued: 'I wonder whether they are as sensitive as mine. Would you care to help me find out?'

The gorgeous girl giggled as she saw me blush but though I was still speechless, she nevertheless sat down on my lap and putting an arm around my neck, pulled my face to her breasts. I threw my arm around her waist and pulled up the frilly garment so that I could see her firm, jutting breasts which were topped with large, nut-brown nipples which I tweaked between my fingers. 'Suck my titties, Salman,' she moaned and I complied, rolling the erect, rubbery flesh between my teeth, nibbling gently on one nipple and then the other as Cherie squirmed in ecstacy. Now in my experience, playing with titties is a prelude to the main event but Cherie needed nothing more as, shaking all over, she spent with a happy little yelp of delight.

'Wait a moment and let me show you something else,' she panted as she returned to the dressing room. My poor prick, which was already threatening to burst out from my trousers, now throbbed uncontrollably as Cherie re-entered the shop naked except for a pair of lace crotchless knickers which made the ravishing girl look even more inviting, especially when she turned her back and bent over the counter, spreading her legs to reveal her glistening wet cunney framed by twin trails of white lace.

Now Chrissie, I have always been true to you, darling, in my fashion. Yes, I've always been true to you darling in my way – but I will have to confess that I found this erotic tableau simply too exciting to bear and I ripped open my trousers and grasping my cock in one hand and wrapping my other arm around her waist so that I could again play with her titties, I eased my knob between her bum cheeks and sank in to the hilt. Wisps of frilly lace tickled my shaft as I pumped in and out of her juicy cunt and what made the love-making even more thrilling was that I could see myself fucking this delicious girl in the long mirror on the wall in front of us. Watching our naked bodies heaving and shoving was so stimulating that I spent very quickly, shooting a torrent of sperm deep inside her longing pussey.

Straightening up, she turned and stood before me, rotating her hips in a tight rhythm. Obviously she had not yet spent a second time so I dropped to my knees and breathed in her musky aroma as I fingered her cunney and began to massage her clitty. 'Ah, c'est magnifique! Continuez, continuez!' she yelped as I licked and lapped around her pussey lips.

Now I placed my lips firmly over her clitty and sucked it into my mouth, with my hands now squeezing her bouncy buttocks and I found the magic button under the fold at the base of Cherie's clitty and twirled my tongue all around it. The faster I vibrated my tongue the more excited she became and she gyrated madly as my darting tongue licked and lapped up the delicious juices which were now running down in a veritable stream from the clinging grooves of her cunney. With each stroke she arched her body in ecstacy, pressing the erect clitty, which was protruding out quite two inches like a tiny cock, against the tip of my flickering tongue.

This oral stimulation soon served its purpose and I brought her off wonderfully. She flooded my face with her juices as she spent exquisitely in great, tumbling spasms.

I had an appointment with my tutor so regretfully I could not take up her kind invitation to go upstairs and fuck in the comfort of her bedroom for the rest of the evening. Now this tale might make you jealous but please note that I also declined the chance to visit Madame Antoinette's shop the next day before Cherie's aunt returned from her brief holiday. And not only have I bought you the negligee and knickers that Cherie modelled but two lovely muslin petticoats with flounces of broderie anglaise and baby ribbon edgings that I am certain you will love to wear — and I hasten to add that these were chosen solely by myself without any help from Cherie!

Despite this erotic encounter, I only have eyes for you, Chrissie, and am counting the hours until we meet again.

All my love,

Salman

I laid down the letter and called over a passing serving girl to refill my cup from the common-room coffeepot which was kept bubbling under a small spirit lamp from after breakfast until midnight.

The maid was a pretty wench who I had not seen before in the college. She could have been no more than eighteen years old, a strawberry-blonde girl who had been blessed with a pert prettiness with wide cornflower-blue eyes, a tiny nose and generously wide red lips through which showed pearly white teeth that sparkled in the bright autumnal light which poured through the large windows.

'Some more coffee, please,' I said, lifting up the

cup to her.

'Thank you, Mr Mountjoy,' she said sweetly.

How did this gorgeous girl know who I was? My fame must have travelled before me, I smiled to myself as I asked her how she knew my name, and the lovely creature coloured slightly as she replied: 'My name is Polly Castle – hasn't my cousin Nancy said anything about my starting work here? She arranged this position for me and Nancy was here a moment ago and pointed you out whilst you were reading your letter. She told me some nice stories about you, Mr Mountjoy.'

'I'm afraid she hasn't mentioned a word to me about her cousin starting work in the college, although I'm not surprised as she would hardly welcome such lovely competition for her favours. But Polly, I sincerely hope that you won't believe everything that Nancy might have told you about me.'

She stole a quick glance down to my groin where my prick, which had stiffened up whilst I was reading Salman's *billet-doux*, was bulging out like a miniature mountain from my lap. 'Well, Nancy did say that you had the sturdiest tool in Balliol,' she said quietly. 'Was this something that I shouldn't believe?'

I looked straight into her large, liquid blue eyes and said: 'I would be happy to let you discover the truth of her observation at any time of your choosing.'

Frankly, I never expected her to take up this lighthearted challenge but to my delighted surprise she immediately replied: 'There's no time like the present as far as I'm concerned. I had just finished my duties when you called me over to pour out some more coffee for you. Oh dear, I don't think there is any left in the pot – I'll have to boil up some more hot water.'

I rose from my chair and winked at her: 'Polly, do *not* put the kettle on! Take off your apron and instead find out if Nancy was telling the truth about my capabilities.'

She hesitated only for a moment and then she gave a cheeky grin. 'Well, why not? I know where your room is, Mr Mountjoy – I'll be there in five minutes.'

'You really don't have to address me as Mr Mountjoy, Polly. All my chums call me Rupert and I trust that we are going to be very close friends – do you agree with me?'

'Oh yes, I do hope so,' she said. 'Very well then – Rupert – I will come upstairs just as soon as I've cleared the rest of the tables.'

All thoughts of spending time in the library had now vanished from my mind and after gathering up my books I ran up the stairs back to my room. I took off my jacket, shoes and socks and was debating whether it would be too forward to take off my trousers when a knock on the door announced Polly's arrival. 'Come in,' I sang out and sure enough, it was the delectable little miss who stepped inside. 'Hello again, Polly, now do sit down on the bed and for a change let me see if I can serve you. Would you care for a glass of wine?'

'Not just now, thank you, but perhaps a little later,' she rejoined as she stood still for a moment and then suddenly, as if remembering why she was here, set to work unhooking her dress and

192

loosening her clothes. I copied her example and in no time at all she stepped out of her garments, naked except for her brief white knickers, whilst I also stripped down to my undershorts with the stiff shaft of my boner standing up like a flagpole against my belly and the rounded red knob poked up over the waistband of my drawers. Polly's bare breasts were simply superb, two proud, firm creamy spheres each tipped with taut crimson titties. My hands were instinctively drawn to these delicious beauties and I reached out and gently squeezed the succulent globes whilst our faces moved slowly forward until our lips melded together into a passionate kiss.

Now the gentleness gave way to a frenzy as, locked together in a tight embrace, we staggered towards the bed and fell upon the mattress, still joined by our mouths. Polly wasted no time and immediately pulled down my drawers and grasped hold of my throbbing tool as she lifted her bum so that I could remove her knickers. I smoothed my hand over the flat expanse of her belly, dimpled as it was with a sweet little navel, like a perfect plain of snow which appeared the more dazzling from the curly locks of silky brown hair that formed a hirsute triangle around her pussey. She opened her legs slightly to allow me a view of the pink chink of her cunney before she climbed up on her knees and moved her hand up and down my blue-veined staff which was now pulsating furiously in expectation of the delights to come.

'What a splendid looking cock!' Polly said admiringly, now holding my engorged truncheon in both hands. 'I like a dick this size which isn't too small for me to feel or too big so that it's hard to take into my cunney. Now I must find out whether this nicely proportioned prick will taste as good as it looks.'

'Please feel free to do so,' I murmured as I lay back and enjoyed the sight of this sensuous girl licking her lips before kissing my knob and thoroughly wetting it with her tongue. She gave my bared helmet a short series of licks before opening her mouth and engulfing it inside her. She closed her lips around it and worked in as much of my shaft as she could, sucking lustily all the while which made me almost faint with sheer delight. As she increased the tempo of her sucking and her teeth scraped the tender cockflesh, she cupped my balls in her hand and this sent me over the edge so that my rigid rod jerked convulsively against the roof of her mouth. In seconds I filled her mouth with a veritable jet of jism which spurted out from my prick and she swallowed the gush of milky love juice until the fountain of frothy seed eased to a mere trickle.

When she had finally drained my twitching tool of the last dribble of my vital essence, Polly looked up at me, my sated prick still between her lips, as she brushed back a lock of hair which had fallen over her face. She bobbed her head up and down for a few moments to keep my prick from sliding back into limpness and kept hold of it in her hand as she scrambled back to lie down again. Then she levered herself up on her arms and looked me full in the face.

'I'm pleased to tell you that your spunk is quite

delicious to swallow, Rupert,' she said happily as she snuggled down beside me, 'and so I award John Thomas ten out of ten on both his looks and the taste of his love liquid.'

'Are there any further tests you would like him to take?'

Polly considered this question with a merry smile thoughtfully before answering: 'Well of course, so far he has only passed the entrance examination. He has yet to attempt his finals which of course means seeing how stylishly he performs in my pussey.'

This was a challenge from which my prick had no intentions of shirking! I said nothing but pulled her closer to me and she responded at once to my embrace and playfully started to rub her soft body against mine. Her mouth was biting at my shoulder and the top of her head was level with my chin. Her nipples traced tiny circles against my chest as she ground herself against me. I gloried in the sensuous warmth which emanated from this divine creature and my cock, now back to its prime state of erectness, found its way unerringly between her legs and her pouting pussey lips were brushing the tip of my knob, frigging my cock up to bursting point.

'May I ride you?' she enquired and I nodded my assent. She wriggled herself between my legs and rising to her knees, she took hold of my iron-hard rod and placed it firmly to the mark. Then Polly pressed herself down and effortlessly her cunt encompassed the entire length of my swollen shaft. She moved sideways a little before settling herself down so that her bottom cheeks sat comfortably upon my thighs. She twitched her shoulders and I watched with awe as her jutting breasts swung free and unencumbered above me. I reached up as she leaned forward, placing her breasts inside my cupped palms and I squeezed and fondled them as she began to bounce up and down upon my own proud stiffstander.

Her red titties rose like twin projectiles as I sucked them into my mouth and Polly leaned further forward, sticking out her tongue, thrusting it deep inside my mouth as I moved my chopper upwards in unison with the downward pistoning of her bum. She adjusted herself slightly so that I could now also feel her silky pussey hair and fleshy clit rubbing along the upper side of my cock, and she rocked backwards and forwards so that her furry mound pressed damply against my own pubic bush.

We matched thrust with counter-thrust until I suddenly had a fancy to fuck Polly doggie-style and gently wrenching my lips from hers I asked if she had any objection to being taken from behind.

'Not in the slightest,' she gasped and obediently turned herself over onto her elbows and knees and raised the delectable soft spheres of her bottom high in the air. Cradling her head on her arm she looked backwards at me with a cheerful smile through the tunnel of her parted thighs. Like her breasts, her bum was beautifully divided and I was tempted to cork my cock into the winking little eye of her rear dimple, but below the glistening damp hair of her pussey hung like an inviting tropical forest. I let my shaft ease its own passage between her bum cheeks which I clutched in my hands. I slid directly inside her and started to fuck her juicy cunney with great relish. I pushed in and pulled out at a steady pace and I looked down with pleasure to see the white shaft of my cock disappearing into the crevice between Polly's buttocks like a gleaming piston of a river steamer.

Deeper and deeper, but still with deliberate speed, I continued to fuck the quivering girl and she moaned and trembled whilst my cock scythed in and out of her squelchy cunt. I held Polly firmly just below her breasts as they swayed from side to side, the nipples touching the sheet as she lowered herself even further.

'Faster! Faster!' she panted and I raised the speed a notch, flashing my prick in and out of her juicy pussey at a quicker rate. But I wanted to make these marvellous moments last as long as possible for I was determined to savour every second of this magnificent joust. So I closed my eyes and tried to keep tight control over my balls which were already threatening to send a foaming gust of spunk hurtling out through my cock. After all, when would I be able to fuck Polly again? Already I would have to find time to service Gillian, Chrissie, Nancy and Beth on a regular basis let alone any other willing girl that came across my path. And I would not be surprised if Nancy ordered her cousin to stay away from my cock if I did not give Nancy enough attention.

However, try as I might, the divine sensations of reaming Polly's slippery love channel soon finished me off and I could not withstand the early familiar feeling of an approaching spend. My balls tightened as, swollen with their load, they slapped against Polly's bum as I pushed inside her pussey one more time.

Polly sensed that the end was near for she suddenly lay down and turned over onto her back, opening her legs to display her sopping cunney. Without pausing I immersed my prick inside her and the clever girl did not close her legs around me but opened her thighs even wider, which allowed me to move my shaft all around her love channel, plumbing any hidden depths which I had not previously touched with my straining knob. Her love juices now poured out from her, soaking the sheet as well as the back of her thighs as the first unstoppable surge of jism coursed its way through my cock and seethed out into her welcoming cunt. This set her off and she twisted in delicious agony as her body was wracked by great shudders which rippled out from her sated pussey as each jolt drove through every fibre of her body.

She rose to meet me as again and again I rammed my spurting cock home and my balls banged vigorously against her bum as now a tide of blissful relief ebbed through me. My pace slowed and the last irregular spasms shook my body as Polly gave one final convulsive heave and then lay very still, her legs and arms splayed out only her breasts still trembling from the frenetic climax which we had experienced.

I slid my now shrivelled joystick out of her and moving down, replaced my cock with my face which I pressed against the wet warmth of her soaking pussey. I breathed in the aroma of our combined spendings and licked at her pussey hair that shone damply around her cunney lips. I licked the inside of her thighs before my head drooped and I rested it upon her pubic mound, thinking how a painter would rejoice in the chance to contrast the silky blackness of Polly's bush against the smooth unblemished whiteness of her belly and thighs.

Now what would be Polly's verdict on my love-making abilities? 'Did you enjoy yourself?' I asked, looking up from my pillow of cunney hair.

'A truly wonderful fuck, Rupert,' she replied lazily, 'and your cock has passed its test with first class honours.' And she then paid me the most tremendous compliment by adding: 'My cousin was right – you have a beautiful cock and what is even more important, you know how to use it.'

'Thank you very much, Polly,' I said with what I hope sounded like a dignified modesty, though inwardly I smirked because those readers blessed with good memories will remember that Gillian Headleigh had paid me a similar compliment after I had fucked her when she had finished telling me the story of the orgy at Lord George Lucas's birthday party. 'There can't be an undergraduate in the whole of Oxford – or Cambridge for that matter – who wouldn't be greatly flattered by such a kind speech, and what makes your words extra special for me is that I have a friend, Frank Folkestone, whose rooms are just across the way, incidentally, who has the most enormous plonker and occasionally, when we have been together with young ladies *au naturel*, I don't mind telling you that once or twice I've been miffed when one of the girls starts talking so admiringly about the huge size of Frank's bell-end.'

'The size of a cock never really matters though I know that all you boys think that an extra couple of inches would come in handy,' said Polly, echoing the words of Gillian and Chrissie after the aforementioned fuck. 'And I admit that the sight of nine inches of proud, rock-hard cockflesh can often excite me. But for me and most of the girls I know it's the look of the owner of the prick which is far more important. We want to see if a man is clean, well turned-out, jolly, generous – and we all have little special likes and dislikes when it comes to physical appearances. For instance, I like a neat, tight bum myself and my cousin Nancy certainly knows what she fancies in a man.'

'And what does she specially like?'

She gave a naughty little giggle. 'Well, come to think of it, there isn't much that Nancy *doesn't* fancy about a man,' she giggled naughtily, 'and in fact she has already warned me about your friend Frank's big cock. I haven't fucked as much as Nancy but one of my best lovers was the local policeman in the little village near Lord Brecklesbury's country house outside Witney, where I worked till Nancy found me a position here when I told her I wanted to live in town. His prick was thick enough but it only stood at less than five inches from base to tip, though he almost always managed to bring me off every time we made love.'

I record Polly's comments *in toto* for as a noted cocksman, I cannot overstress the importance of her observation which had been mirrored of course by Gillian and Chrissie as well as by my very first fuck, the delicious Diana Wigmore, who had always impressed upon me the importance of never worrying about the dimensions of my equipment or about the fact that at times my young prick might jump up to attention for no apparent reason or that it might obstinately refuse to swell up when required – say when the lovely girl you have been wooing finally consents to place her hand inside your trousers!

However, it was time for Polly and I to get dressed for she had further chores to get through whilst I knew that I would find myself in real trouble if I did not make my way post-haste to the library. I kissed the charming girl goodbye and we made an arrangement to see each other the next week when to her great joy I promised to take her to the first house of the music hall and on to a café for some supper.

For the second time that morning I gathered my books together and told myself that nothing would stop me from going to the library except a visit to the college from His Majesty, King Edward VII, Defender of the Faith, Emperor of India 'and all stations south of Birmingham,' I muttered to myself as I raced down the stairs, determined to put in at least an hour's work before luncheon.

But it was not to be! For who should I meet at the foot of the stairs but Beth Randall and Esme Dyotte, the two girls with whom Barry Jacobs and myself shared a splendid night's fucking courtesy of our host Mr Waterbrick of The Cat and Pigeons.

'Hello, stranger!' squealed Esme. 'We haven't

seen you for so long that Beth and I decided to see for ourselves that you were still in the land of the living.'

'Or to ensure that you had not been rusticated *[temporarily expelled from the University for bad behaviour – Editor]* which we thought more likely,' added Beth with a roguish grin.

Oh no, I groaned inwardly, as the wise words of Mustapha Pharte, the perhaps unfortunately named Oxford-based disciple of the Indian philosopher Tagore, whose teachings were beginning to influence very many young people at this time, rushed through my brain – 'Take care that an overindulgence of your favourite pastime (in my case, chasing pussey) does not overtax your strength'. Now it was not difficult to see from the glint in their eyes that both girls had not come to my rooms simply to pass the time of day, but I had spent almost all the previous night fucking Marianne and if that were not enough, pretty little Polly Castle had twice emptied my balls. Even if I agreed to comply with the wishes of these two lovely ladies, would I be physically able to do so?

'Well come on, Rupert, aren't you going to invite us to your room to show us your etchings?' said Esme impatiently.

There was nothing for it but to smile and wave the girls upstairs, I reasoned, for the girls would rightly consider it the height of rudeness to spurn the offer of a freely offered fuck.

'It will be my pleasure to entertain you both,' I said with as much enthusiasm as I could muster. 'Though I have no paintings to show you, perhaps I can offer you a glass of wine or some other refreshment.'

'Or maybe both?' enquired Esme wickedly, slipping her arm in mine as we walked back upstairs to my rooms.

'Don't be too impatient, Esme – we'll begin with a glass of wine,' said Beth, settling herself down on the small sofa whilst I hung up their coats and busied myself selecting a decent bottle of white wine from the icebox, which incidentally was one of the first purchases I made in Oxford and is still in full working order.

'I'm afraid that I don't keep any champagne here, Beth,' I apologised, 'but let's open this bottle of Vernaccia from Sardinia your cousin Diana Wigmore sent me after she returned from her Grand Tour this summer.'

'I'm sure it will be lovely,' said Beth. 'More and more people are coming to realise that many Italian vineyards produce wine of an excellent quality. We do not look at Italian wines as seriously as we should because the Italians regard wine as something to be drunk and enjoyed rather than talked and written about like the French, who have cleverly conjured up a mystique of unique quality about their wares, from fashion to liqueurs.

'But it's funny that you should bring up Diana's name, Rupert. I had a letter from her the other day and she asks me to send you her love. When she was in Italy this summer, you know, she took a course in painting with the famous Professor Arturo Volpe in Milan.'

'Did she really? Even I have heard of the great

Arturo Volpe. He is one of the top teachers in Europe and he must have thought very highly of Diana's work to allow her to join one of his classes.'

'Yes, I suppose so,' said Beth slowly, 'though I think Diana helped matters along by offering to pose nude for his students. She wrote to me what happened when she finished one session and all the students had filed out of the room, leaving herself together with Professor Volpe. Look, I have her letter with me – would you care to read it?'

She rummaged in her bag and passed me a couple of sheets of paper from it. Good grief! I had only just finished perusing Salman's sensual epistle to Chrissie, but I was curious to read how Diana had managed to wriggle herself into one of the best master classes in Europe, so I took the letter and sat down next to Beth and began to read. I skipped through the text until she came to the incident Beth had mentioned, and readers will note that Diana indeed had used all her wiles to secure a place with the great man.

So when the last student had left, I slipped off the pedestal and made my way across to Professor Volpe who was sitting at his desk. Luckily he speaks excellent English (for my Italian is disgracefully poor) and I asked him what time I would be required the next day, and whilst he was replying I pretended to see a coin on the floor and I bent down to pick it up. This gave him an excellent view of my bottom which was only inches away from his face. I looked up and saw that he was appreciative of the two soft globes and so when I straightened up I said that I had been mistaken. Then I affected to trip forwards and fell across him, taking good care that my breasts fell nicely into his hands.

At first he was embarrassed but I quickly made clear my intentions by taking his hands and pressing them to my naked nipples. He looked startled for a moment but then he responded and we were soon engaged in a long, lingering kiss. I felt for his cock but there seemed nothing stirring in his lap so I slid off him and stood directly in front of him. Then I opened my legs and I began to stroke my cunney through the blonde silky bush of my mound. I slipped a finger into the moistening crack and started to rub myself off.

Professor Volpe obviously enjoyed watching me masturbate as I caressed my breasts seductively with one hand, tweaking my titties lasciviously, whilst finger-fucking myself with the other. He unbuckled his trousers and pulled them down to reveal his now hard, stiffstanding shaft. I looked down at his prick which was of no great size but of quite a thick girth and decided to stop the show. Instead, I dropped to my knees to suck upon his knob and run my fingernails lightly up and down the veiny length. He groaned with delight when I switched to his ballsack which with one gulp I had in my mouth, and I massaged his thick staff up to its throbbing, twitching peak whilst I sucked his heavy balls.

Before long we found ourselves on the couch upon which I had been reclining for the students and I moved round, my lips still around his cock, so that my cunney was above his head, and as I lowered myself down he wiggled his tongue all

around my dripping slit. By this time we were both
moaning with genuine pleasure and I urged him to
move round and get on top of me. When he was in
position I took his shaft in my hands and guided him
into my longing love-channel.

He fucked me very nicely for about a couple of
minutes until he shot a great spurt of spunk into my
honeypot. I didn't spend myself but this pleasant
little fuck was very enjoyable and certainly did the
trick as far as getting me into his classes was
concerned. In fact, I would never have let anyone
fuck me simply to further myself in some way. If
Professor Volpe had asked me to suck his cock, I
would have been delighted to comply with such or
any other erotic request as I regarded it as an honour
to be fucked by the great man.

I passed the letter back to Beth who looked at
me curiously and said: 'Rupert, you look
somewhat pale and tense. Are you feeling
unwell?'

'Yes, I'm quite fit, thank you, but I do feel a little
tired even though I overslept this morning and
truthfully, I'm also getting very worried about all
the work which I have to plough through and
how I am going to fit it all in with my social
arrangements.'

'Oh, you must never let business interfere with
pleasure,' chirped up Esme. 'You're probably just
feeling out of sorts because you woke up late. My
granny always says if you lose an hour in the
morning you'll spend the rest of the day looking
for it.'

But Beth could see that I was really out of sorts

and after we had drunk our wine she whispered something to Esme who nodded her head and smiled at me, saying: 'I have a couple of small errands to perform, Rupert. Will you excuse me for an hour or so? But Beth will stay and she'll help you relax.'

What was all this about? Beth soon answered my unspoken question by taking me by the hand and guiding me onto the bed. 'No, I don't want you to fuck me,' she said. 'At least, not until I've managed to clear your mind and refresh your body by giving you an Oriental massage. I've always been a great believer in the principle of *mens sana in corpore sano [a healthy mind in a healthy body – Editor]* and I promise you that you'll feel so much better afterwards. I hope you'll let me try this out on you because you don't look your usual sparkling self.'

'I do need toning up in some way,' I admitted sheepishly, 'so I'd be more than grateful if you'd give me, a what did you call it?'

'An Oriental massage, Rupert. I was shown the secrets of the art by a friend who has spent several years in Hong Kong and if I say so myself, I picked up the technique extremely well.'

'I'm sure you have, Beth. So how do we start the ball rolling?'

'Lie down and let me help you undress,' she instructed as she sat down on the bed and unlaced my shoes. I unbuttoned my shirt and unbuckled my belt whilst she pulled off my shoes and socks. I arched my back to allow her to ease my trousers and drawers over my bottom and in a trice I was naked as nature intended. 'Now it's my turn,' she said softly, stepping out of her shoes. Then she slipped off her blouse before unhooking her skirt and letting it fall to the floor. She sat on the bed and peeled off her stockings and lifted her chemise over her head to reveal her bouncy white breasts with their pert ripe nipples which almost appeared to be stiffening as she wriggled out of her knickers. She smoothed her hand across her fluffy blonde bush and I reached up to place my hands upon her breasts.

But she stepped back a pace and said: 'Not yet, Rupert, you're not yet in trim. First, I want you to turn over and lie on your tummy.' I sighed but obeyed her command and Beth jumped up on the bed. On her knees between my parted legs, she placed her hands on the back of my neck and began to massage me, not too fiercely but at a slow, sensual pace, starting at my neck and working her way down my back, over my buttocks and thighs until she came to my ankles. She surprised me with the strength of her fingers but I must say that my muscles relaxed under the firm pressure of my skilled masseuse.

She worked her way back up to my neck and then began to run her fingertips ever so lightly down my body. When her fingers reached the small of my back she slid her hands back and forth across my buttocks, then down the outsides of my legs to my feet and back up the insides until she came to my balls which she softly caressed from behind. Naturally, my cock rose up to greet Beth's hands even though she did not actually touch my shaft.

After a minute or so she told me to turn over

and I rolled over on to my back. 'Keep your arms down by your side,' she said as I moved my hands to cup her gorgeous breasts which dangled so invitingly when she leaned forward to repeat this fabulous massage. So I simply closed my eyes and enjoyed the feel of Beth's hands pressing and kneading my muscles and though my stiffstander was waving frantically at her she kept her hands away from the throbbing pole. But relief was soon at hand for once she had given me the soft butterfly touch of her fingertips, she lowered her mop of silky blonde hair and planted a smacking wet kiss on my lips. With difficulty I restrained myself and kept my arms resting on the eiderdown as she worked her tongue down my body, stopping briefly to circle my nipples before at last descending to my aching cock.

She licked all round my helmet and then sucked in as much of my straining shaft as she could manage, stroking my length with one hand and teasing my balls with the other. She opened her mouth and sucked in almost all my cock until it touched her throat. Up and down, up and down bobbed her head until I almost fainted away with pleasure. Once she had thoroughly anointed my pulsing prick, Beth climbed aboard for a ride. She leaned over so that her stalky red nipples brushed my chest and this time she raised no objection as I slid my hands under them and rubbed her titties against my palms. This was a short, sharp fuck but memorable for its intensity for her cunney muscles clung deliciously to my cock as it slid up and down inside her tight, wet sheath. All too soon, the spunk came rushing through my twitching tool and with a low growl, I sent a mighty burst of hot, seething jism upwards into her eager nook. Gush after gush spurted deep inside as Beth's climax followed almost immediately.

'There, do you feel better now?' she enquired with a smile as we lay in each other's arms.

'I should say so,' I said enthusiastically. 'Let's finish that bottle of wine and have another little fuck before luncheon.'

'What a splendid idea!' said a voice from the doorway and we looked over to see that Esme had returned. 'I'll just undress and then I'll fill our glasses,' she added as she took off her coat.

Esme was as good as her word and the three of us lay naked on the bed, drinking and laughing until Esme took hold of my semi-stiff love trunk and rubbed it between her palms until it stood up to attention, waving slightly as Beth and Esme knelt down in front of it and took turns to lick my shaft. Esme then gobbled my purple knob before taking about three inches of my cock into her mouth. As she sucked lustily on my delighted tadger, Beth kissed and licked my ballsack and then the girls swapped places and Beth lapped at my bared knob with the tip of her tongue, savouring the salty pre-cum which had already formed around the 'eye'. I thrust my slippery shaft upwards between her lips as she jammed my cock between them.

There was time for just one more turnabout as Esme took my pulsating pole inside her mouth and she slid her lips as far down my shaft as possible, feeling my wiry pubic hair tickle her nose. She sneezed and Beth left her exquisite palating of my hairy ballsack to say gaily: 'Esme dear, Lady Scadgers' Book of Etiquette expressly states that one should never sneeze with one's mouth full of cock.'

I thought that Esme would choke with laughter but she sucked away vigorously until the girls finished me off and she swallowed my spunk in great gulps, pulling me hard into her mouth as I delivered the contents of my balls in a fierce squirt of white frothy cream. They licked up the last drains of my spend together until my prick had been totally milked and my shaft began to shrink back to its normal size.

Beth and Esme would liked to have continued playing three-in-a-bed – who was the dolt who laid down the old law about the female being the weaker of the sexes? – but I was saved by the resonant sound of the dining-room gong and I invited the girls to quickly dress themselves and join me for luncheon.

By good fortune Mike Beattie and his friend and fellow-Scot Allan Campbell were taking luncheon in college that day and I took the opportunity of introducing the Caledonian duo to Beth and Esme. When the girls left us to wash their hands I hurriedly explained my predicament to the two Scottish lads. 'I may be wrong but in all probability Beth and Esme are expecting to be fucked this afternoon and frankly, I'm just not capable of performing any more till tonight at the earliest. Would you kindly offer your cocks to the girls if need be?'

'With pleasure, Rupert,' said Mike warmly.

'Shall we inform the ladies that our pricks are at their disposal or would you prefer to tell them yourself?'

'It's probably best to play it by ear,' I advised the eager lads who were only too willing to please the two insatiable girls if required. 'I think you'll know well enough if your services are required.'

'It's a pity I'm not wearing my kilt or they could see something to tickle their fancy without too much bother,' commented Allan, but as it turned out, the four of them got on splendidly and after polishing off two bottles of the college claret, we were all feeling very merry. Esme asked Allan what was his field of study and when he replied that he was taking a degree in English Literature, she made us all roar with laughter when she said she also enjoyed poetry and, when being told that Allan's home city was Dundee, recited the following limerick:

There was a young man of Dundee,
Who one night went out on the spree;
He wound up his clock
With the tip of his cock,
And buggered himself with the key.

'I hope I have not offended you,' she said, but Allan shook his head and replied:

'Of course not, Esme, would you like to hear another rhyme about my home town?

A pretty young girl from Dundee
Went down to the river to pee.
A man in a punt
Put his hand on her cunt,
By God! How I wish it was me.'

'It must be the influence of McGonagall *[William McGonagall (1830-1902) was a deluded Dundee-born writer of bathetic doggerel of poor scansion who imagined himself to be a divinely inspired poet – Editor]* which makes people laugh when they find a Dundonian who is studying poetry,' said Michael Beattie.

'Probably so,' said Esme, 'but tell me, from where do you hail, Michael?'

'From Perth, another city on the silvery Tay, as McGonagall might say.'

'Very good,' said Esme, finishing off her glass of the very passable college claret. 'Then I dedicate a verse to you – how about:

> *Mike Beattie who hails from Perth*
> *Had the biggest balls e'er seen on earth.*
> *They grew to such size*
> *That one won a prize*
> *And goodness knows what they were worth.'*

Perhaps it was as well that a two shilling *[ten pence! – Editor]* bribe to Mrs Woodway, who supervised mid-week luncheons, afforded us the luxury of dining in a small private room off the main hall. When it was time to pass the port we were all rather flushed and certainly far merrier than when we sat down to begin our meal. This free and easy atmosphere afforded me the opportunity to ask Beth if she and Esme would agree to my leaving the party. 'Please don't be offended but if I don't get on with my work I really will have good cause to worry and not even your delightful Oriental rub down will be able to help me – not even if you massage Professor

Webb and my tutor!'

'It's quite all right, Rupert,' she said kindly. 'You run along – Esme and I will be well taken care of by these two strapping Scotsmen, won't we boys?'

Allan and Michael chorused their agreement and so I kissed the two girls goodbye and walked back slightly unsteadily to my quarters. But after a brief rest, dear reader, at the third time of trying I finally managed to find my way to the library where I spent the rest of the afternoon with my nose to the grindstone!

But no, I cannot conclude these memoirs with an economy of truth! I did take a ten minute break at four o'clock to see if the girls had stayed with Allan and Michael. I left my books and papers on the library desk and made my way up to Michael Beattie's rooms. I thought I could hear some familiar sounds but as I discovered as I tried slowly to turn the handle of his door, he had taken the sensible precaution of locking the happy group out of sight of prying eyes.

Now if he reads this manuscript, Mike Beattie will discover for the first time, that what went on that afternoon did not go unseen! For as I cursed Mike for being so careful, who should I meet on the landing but Nancy, who had also been drawn to the scene by the muffled cries and giggles that emanated from (as he is now entitled to be known, having joined the Scots Guards after graduation) Major Beattie's bedroom.

Carefully, she unlocked the door with her skeleton key and I pushed the door slightly ajar so that we could see inside – and what we saw was worth the effort we had made to view the lewd girls and boys!

Allan Campbell lay sprawled naked but *hors de combat* on the carpet, fast asleep, with his prick dangling over his left thigh as he lay dead to the world. But Mike Beattie was obviously made of sterner stuff for he was engaged in an interesting situation with Beth and Esme on the bed. Beth was on her back and Esme was lying on top of her so that the two girls' tummies and titties were pressed together with Esme's legs stretched out to encompass her friend's limbs. But behind her, Mike had climbed up and Nancy and I saw him guide his thick cock in the crevice between Esme's luscious buttocks.

'Is he fucking her up the bum or in her cunney?' whispered Nancy as the broad shouldered Scot eased his knob into one of Esme's orifices.

Mike unknowingly answered her question by groaning aloud: 'Esme, what a lovely juicy cunney you have, my prick is sliding into it like a knife through butter. And as he fucked her from behind, Esme sucked upon Beth's erect rosy titties as she pushed a thigh up against the blonde girl's pussey and began to rub it sensually against her silky fleece. Their gentle caresses rapidly acquired an urgency as the lusty Mr Beattie slewed his sturdy prick in and out of Esme's moist, yielding love channel and in turn she sucked furiously upon Beth's firm nipples, all the while massaging those divinely full high breasts.

'Oooh! I've come!' squawked Esme.

'You lucky girl – then may I have Mike's cock inside me to finish me off?' Beth responded.

'Certainly you may, and I'm sure Mike has no objection,' said Esme graciously and she wriggled off her friend to let the handsome young Scot mount Beth and place the tip of his glistening cock inside her.

'Aaaah! That's the ticket – slide all your fat prick inside me,' cried Beth as she raised her hips sharply to meet his initial thrust, forcing more of his shaft inside her, though it slid out as she fell back on the pillow. On stiffened arms, he teased her cunney by only inserting a couple of inches of his sizeable length but then with a growl he drove down and she took in the entire veiny staff as their pubic hairs entwined together. She wrapped her legs around his waist as Esme kindly slid a pillow under her hips to intensify the pressure of his cock against her pubes. Beth thrashed around, caught up in a wild ecstasy as she spent again and again before Mike's body went rigid and he trembled all over before releasing his flow of sticky white love cream.

Esme now re-entered the fray by pulling Mike off and rubbing his twitching tool between her hands until she was satisfied that it stood as high and firm as before he shot his load. Then rolling him upon his back, she straddled him and with a single downwards motion impaled herself upon his throbbing tool.

With long, lingering strokes she slid her hungry pussey up and down the towering pole and Mike used one hand to play with Esme's breasts and the other to continue to finger-fuck Beth's cunney as she lay with her legs wide open, crooning with glee as sparks of excitement from her big spend continued to excite her.

At this point Nancy and I closed the door quietly and the little minx squeezed my cock which, as may well be imagined, was bulging out from my trousers. 'Time for a quickie?' she suggested but I knew that I had to decline.

However, I did not give the real reason for my decision not to slip into an empty bedroom with her, but said in as regretful a tone as I could muster: 'Oh Nancy, I'd adore fucking you but we won't have enough time to make love as fully as you deserve. Come to my room later this evening and we'll be able to relax and make love without having to keep one eye on the clock.'

This satisfied the sweet girl though I knew that my cock needed a longer rest from all this frenetic activity. Still, after several years engagement in a similar routine, I can report that despite the warnings of certain jealous gentlemen, it is still in fine fettle and shows no sign of wear and tear!

ENVOI

HERE I CONCLUDE THIS ACCOUNT OF my first term at my old *alma mater*. But I will pen a frank, uncensored narrative of my further adventures with Chrissie, Beth and some new girls and boys who were to cross my path during my stay midst the dreaming spires of Oxford. Gad! How lucky I was to have enjoyed the company of such a merry and uninhibited crew during these formative years.

My thanks to them and finally of course to you, dear reader, who I sincerely hope has enjoyed reading my recollections of what some prudes might call a mis-spent youth. But I don't regret a single day of the time spent at the Varsity, especially (as was not always the case afterwards as will be seen in my next volume of intimate memoirs) as I dallied with impunity so many times in beds which were not my own without any unfortunate consequences.

Till then, *au revoir*.

TO BE CONTINUED